Redwoods Rampage

A Supernatural Western Thriller

Chuck Buda

La Cigolli Publishing

Copyright © 2022 by Chuck Buda

Cover Design by Phil Yarnall at SMAYdesign.com

All rights reserved.

No portion of this book may be reproduced in any form without written permission from the publisher or author, except as permitted by U.S. copyright law. Any resemblance between the people in this book and people in the real world is purely coincidental and unintended.

Dedicated to Thomas Barragan

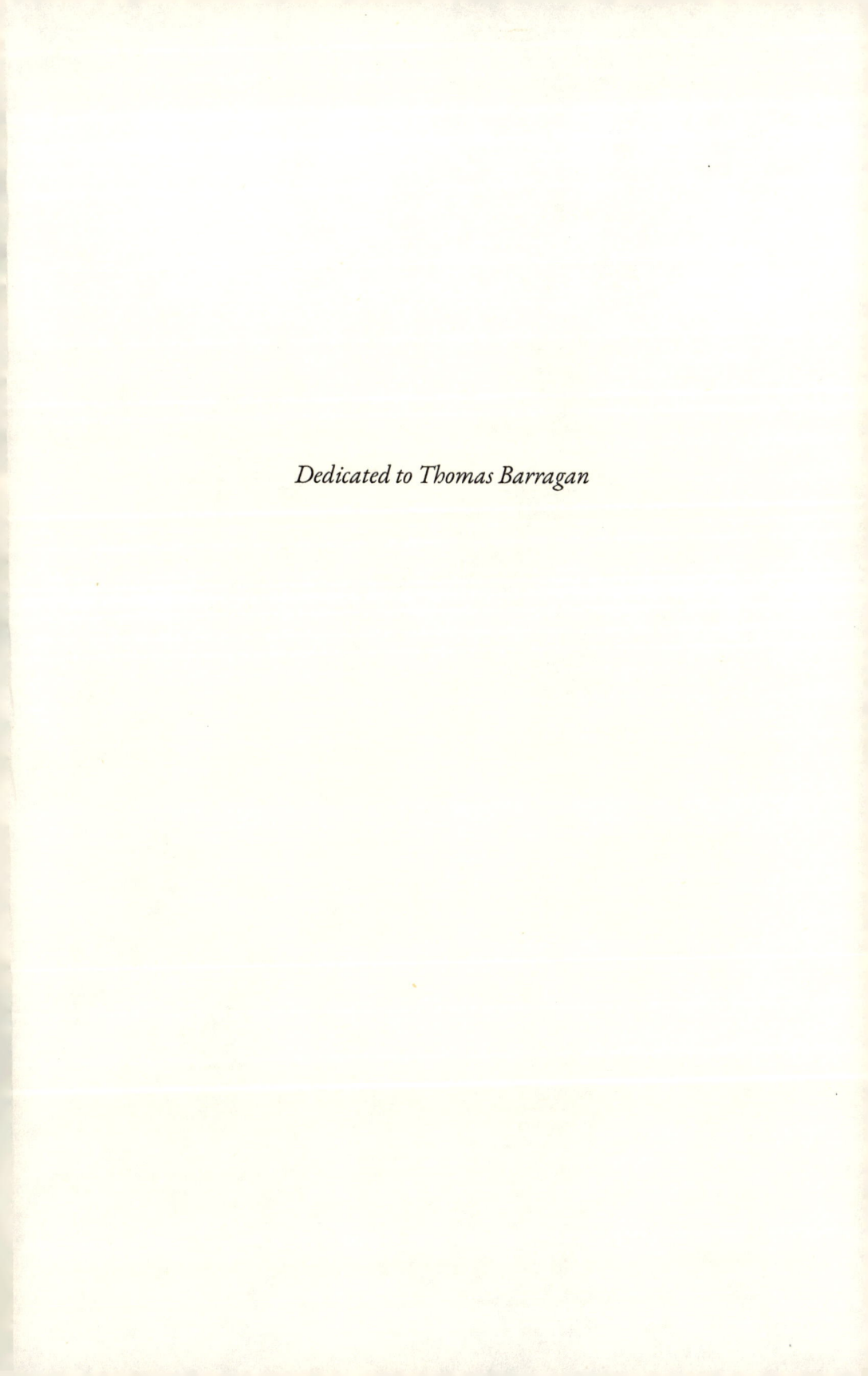

Chapter One

Markus Hedman had spent years combing the hills of northern California and Oregon. He had the fever and he hoped to sate the hunger before others traveled west. He had been duped into buying phony maps and investing in empty claims.

But now his luck had changed.

After years of ignoring his own health and hygiene, Markus had unearthed a solid vein of gold. He laughed at the heavens. A gem of sparkling ore held aloft, Markus felt the sun bake the filth upon his blackened teeth. He kissed the stone and turned it over and over in his sandy palm. Never in his fifty-two years had Markus witnessed such beauty. Even the pastor's wife, Eunice, looked dull and unattractive when compared to the rock he grasped at this moment.

Markus tucked the gold into his pocket, feeling the warmth glow through the fabric. His jagged fingernails clawed into the opening. His trowel sat at his knee, no longer important to uncovering the vast riches he had dreamed of all these years. As he dug deeper into the cool soil beneath the boulder that had hidden the vein, a scream rattled the bones in his skin.

He craned his neck above the engorged roots of the redwood tree. All signs of life had fallen dormant. Markus' ears rang with the deafening silence that had recently been filled with squawks, chirps, and whistles. Even the clouds above hid behind the blazing heat of the sun in fear of what signaled a return to the forest.

A swish of leaves to his left startled Markus.

His eyes frantic with fright.

An enormous limb crashed to the ground, sending a plume of dirt and sticks into the ray of sunlight that had broken through a hole in the canopy.

Markus gasped, nearly swallowing his own tongue.

Another scream, so loud it caused his organs to rattle inside his chest. Markus shot to his feet. His fingers traced the rock in his pocket, protecting what he had rightfully uncovered.

Excessive panic surged through his veins. Markus found himself fleeing before he knew why he was on the run. He felt something bearing down on him even though he could not see it.

The forest behind him crashed and crunched. Markus ran like a child playing tag. The thing that stalked him nipped at his heels. His lungs burned in an effort to pump as much oxygen into his blood as it would be required to carry him out of harm's way.

Markus tripped on a hidden bump in the hill. His feet flew over his head as the cottony blue sky circled above and below him. With a thud that sapped his lungs of the last tendrils of air, Markus stared into the sky. The earth beneath him shook and bounced. Each step nearer lifted him higher off the ground. From the right, a storm cloud bigger than the tornadoes he had seen as a child in Oklahoma blotted out the forces of life above.

What Markus stared at above him could only be the sight of something from the depths of Hell that the pastor ranted about on Sunday mornings. The face, human and yet inhuman, came into focus. The eyes.

A long string of drool lost its perch from the creature's lips and splashed on Markus' chest.

"No."

The word was little more than a whisper as he had no air left in his body. A massive, hairy arm reached from a mile high and grasped at Markus' wrist. It growled and ripped his arm above its head.

Markus' tongue lapped at the sky as it screamed in horror, a witness to his severed limb. The creature swung the bloody appendage downward like a hammer in search of a nail. The torn flesh slapped the top of Markus' head, dazing him. Subconsciously, Markus rolled onto his side and scrambled back into a full sprint. Down an arm, Markus thought how odd it felt to run without the help of two arms to propel him forward.

The hot breath of the monster just steps behind him. He listened to the beast taking two steps for every six to ten that he took. As he ran with every ounce of horror in his system, the thing that hunted him hardly needed to walk quickly.

It caught him by the back of his neck in a tight squeeze of its fist. Markus' neck collapsed like a sack of powder with no shape or substance. The greasy head flopped backwards with no more support to keep it perched on his shoulders. Markus' body continued to run a few more paces before the message had reached the rest of the extremities.

Markus was dead.

The hairy monster stood above, whooping three times in a defined cadence. In the distance to the west, a response of three knocks upon a tree trunk. To the south, three higher pitched whoops answered the call.

Grasping a leg by the ankle, the wild man dragged Markus Hedman across the forest floor. A trail of matted down grass and dirt followed the creature as it went deeper into the dark recesses of the forest. More knocks and whoops from different directions told the monster the others were on their way. Soon, the family would be reunited and dinner would be served.

The monster owned the forest and refused to share its home with the men who brought a scourge upon the land. The wild man had witnessed the destruction humans had levied from the east clear across the Rockies into the west. Each time it had erected its barriers to their expansion, the wild man had been forced to flee farther from its origin. With the sea nearby, the creature had decided to make a final stand against extinction. It had made deals in the past with the red man, to be left to its own culture. But there was no communion with white man.

Markus Hedman's skull came apart as it got snagged along the roots and underbrush, disappearing like the wind into the densely populated woods of the Shasta Mountains. What had once been visible along the landscape now faded into the background as the hairy man became one with the redwoods.

Chapter Two

James scooted Carson along with a gentle prod. They had been hiking since before daybreak and James knew Carson had grown weary. His own feet throbbed inside dirty boots. James curled his toes to bring some relief, thinking about a new pair of boots. He promised himself that would be his first investment in Northern California.

"I'm tired, James."

Carson's eyebrows slid up his sweaty forehead in a desperate plea for respite. James nodded at Carson to continue forward.

Inside the valley, between two snow-capped peaks, any semblance of a refreshing breeze had dissipated with the noon sun. The miners dripped with perspiration as they trudged toward the bend in the foothills. Pack mules grunted under the weight of their loads, each beast piled high with canvas tents, tools, chuck boxes and supplies. One man with a switch slapped at the rear of one of the mules.

As the travelers rounded the bend, an enormous forest filled their vision. The trees, many as wide as whole city blocks, stretched high into the clouds. James watched Carson's jaw drop.

"Whoa." Carson halted and pulled his hat off for a better look. His neck craned as far back as it could without snapping in half.

James bumped into Carson, distracted with his own amazement.

"Keep moving. We ain't there yet."

A young man with a protruding Adam's apple and a narrow head perched on a thin neck groused at them. James stared at the young man.

"Move it."

Before James could decide whether to box the young man's ears or obey his command, a rotund miner enveloped in a cloud of dust stepped forward. He clutched James' arm and tugged him forward with the strength of one hundred horses. James allowed the man to lead him forward. He did not want to fight two men over a small slight.

The burly miner released James and quickened his pace towards the front of the pack. Carson wheezed, his little legs doubling the work of the men just to keep up.

"Are those trees real, James?"

"Sure are, Carson." James shielded his eyes to peer at the leafy tops of the gigantic woods. "I bet we could have made some fantastic forts with these things, huh?"

Carson grinned and nodded. "We would hided and nevered be finded by anyone."

The long line of miners and mules slowed down as they began a winding ascent through the redwood forest. Huge ferns passed along a delicate breeze underneath the shady trees, bringing happiness to all the travelers. The trunks of the trees reflected ambient light from its waxy surface. Gazing directly above, James and Carson tried to imagine setting atop the highest limbs. The view must stretch for thousands of miles from such a height.

Carson gasped.

"I don't feel good."

James knelt before his friend. "Are you going to be sick?" James glanced about. "Plenty of privacy in here if you need to let it out."

Carson shivered. He shook his head violently. "No. I'm not sick."

"Then what's the matter?"

CHAPTER 2

James watched the last group of miners pass by. He squeezed Carson's shoulders, hoping to get his buddy moving before someone else hollered at them for not keeping up.

"A monster."

James huffed. He pushed Carson back into the root-covered trail. "Ain't no monsters, Carson."

Carson insisted something bad followed them. He argued he felt the monster's anger in his head. James bit his tongue against further upsetting Carson. He wanted to quell Carson's overactive imagination but James decided it would be easier to ignore the silliness.

As they caught up to the back end of the train, the young man with the bobbing throat and skinny neck stood with his arms crossed. Green eyes glared from under reddened eyebrows. James forced a smile to appease the hostility. James held Carson's hand to keep him moving.

"I hope you work better than you walk."

James squeezed Carson's hand so tight the boy howled in pain.

"I'll be watching you two closely. If I don't like what I see then you won't collect a paycheck."

Releasing Carson's fist, James squared off with the red-headed turkey neck. "You don't need to worry about my work ethic. Or his." James nodded over his shoulder.

The young man stepped inside the brim of James' hat. His stale breath wrinkled James' nose.

"We'll see about that." The green eyes darted back and forth like a hunter scanning the landscape for movement. "Keep up. Now. Or drop out. Mr. Johnson."

James maintained the intimate distance, not wishing to show fear. "How do you know my name?"

The young man finally stepped back. He smirked like a child hiding a secret. "I know everyone's name in my company."

James' shoulders slumped. "You're not Mr. Phillips."

"Technically, I am. My name is Remus. Remus Phillips."

Carson tugged at James' belt loop as if he needed immediate attention.

"Mr. Phillips is my father. He owns Phillips Mining Company. But I run the outfit." Remus spat. "I'm the boss. And you work for me. Until you don't."

James choked on a ball of saliva as his mouth dried out. He disliked Remus and knew this would be the start of many head-to-head battles. James decided to bite his tongue for now. The boys needed the job and the money until they settled into California.

But Remus would get his, James silently vowed.

Carson tugged James' belt loop so hard it nearly tore free of the dungarees. James lowered his head and shuffled Carson up the knotted trail, leaving Remus Phillips behind. Carson insisted James listen to him.

"Pay attention."

James grimaced. "What now?"

Carson choked on his words like he had lost all his breath running for miles. He repeated the tale of some monster trying to scare them away. Carson felt the monster staring at him and waiting to take him away. James scolded Carson.

"Knock it off, Carson. We're in enough trouble as it is without your stupid imagination. Besides, monsters only come out at night. Remember?"

Carson's lips trembled. His eyes glared around every tree and beneath each fern. "This monster is different, James. It's not pretended."

James shushed Carson as Remus Phillips passed them at a quicker pace. He glowered along his nose as he stepped beyond them. James gritted his teeth.

Two things to deal with already.

Remus.

And Carson.

Chapter Three

Carson stopped chipping into the wall to inspect the blisters breaking out along his palms. James thought of offering consolation but the twinge in his back diverted him. The long trail from Sacramento to Orick had been completed with a quick setup of the encampment before beginning the arduous mining activity. Remus Phillips told them to start working that same night.

No rest.

Remus reasoned they had lost time along the trail and needed to do whatever necessary to meet the original deadline for excavating the first mine.

"Your body won't know it's nighttime once you're down the hole anyway."

James picked at a fresh vein with miniscule specks of gold. He wondered how long they would be forced to stay on before getting much needed sleep. The beefy miner who had saved James from tussling with Remus crowded nearby. He yanked the pickaxe from James' hands and demonstrated how to make more efficient strokes.

"Like this. And this. See?" The man's hat had a chunk torn from the front brim. It looked as if some animal had taken a bite of the felt cloth, leaving a ragged edge. His beard grew close to his wrinkled eyes. Only a bulbous nose jutting from the grayed hair on his face. "Easier on the back. And quicker payload. Here."

The pick had been shoved back into James' hands, nearly knocking him off his feet. James felt the strength in the older man's body would be something to be reckoned with. It reminded him of George's stature and power.

"Show me."

James hurried to imitate the new method before the geezer got angry with him. Satisfied James had understood his lesson, the burly man strode towards another group of miners. A Chinese worker shoveled the loosened soil along the floor into several buckets at his feet. James watched incredulously at the speed of the small man's movement.

"You work. No look."

James blinked, unaware he had paused to stare. The Chinese fellow barked as he worked.

"Boss man whip. You work. No whip."

As James returned to chipping into the wall, the Chinaman hooked four buckets filled with earth onto a curved stick. He hoisted the stick along his shoulders, behind his neck, and hurried toward the mineshaft. James suddenly felt like a child among men. He thought he had seen powerful men in the past but the miners made all other men appear soft.

"How's it going over here?"

James flinched. The sudden shock of a deep voice scared him almost out of his boots.

"Good. All good."

A large palm slapped James across the back, nearly tumbling him into the wall.

"Glad to hear it. The name is Skunk."

James accepted the outstretched hand. The size of a bear claw, it engulfed James' flesh. His eyes watered at the extreme body odor emanating from the man's personal space. James tried to determine if the man was named because of his smell or the large streak of gray hair along the right side of his head. Skunk's hair stood wild in every direction like a porcupine's quills.

CHAPTER 3

"If you need anything, just give me a holler. I act as a sorta foreman around here. The boss doesn't think so but without me he wouldn't have the trust of these men."

James wished to inquire if they would be getting rest soon but thought he would sound like a whiny child so he dismissed the question.

"I'm James. He's my brother, Carson." James aimed the pick at his friend who crouched low along the wall.

"Where you from, James?"

Before responding, James believed it would be best to keep his true identity a secret. And that included his home. "Pretty much everywhere."

Skunk guffawed with a deep base tremor in his throat. "We get that a lot around these parts. Everyone running from someone or someplace." He glanced down at Carson. "Keep an eye on that boy. Men in these towns can't be trusted around weaker folks. Causes them to do things a man should never do."

He began to move further down the mine, ruffling Carson's hair as he passed. "And if the mean men don't come after the boy, the wild man of the woods will for sure."

Skunk bellowed fits of laughter as he disappeared past the glow of lanterns near them. His tremulous voice wafting up from the darkness like a ghost.

James shuddered. He refused to give in to such notions of Carson being kidnapped. Too many times, Carson had taken the brunt of violence and James' eyes watered with renewed protective promises and love.

The Chinese man returned with empty buckets. He slumped them to the floor and glared around his feet.

"You work more. I carry. No whip."

James worked with extra gusto after the short break. He chipped at the wall as the immigrant worker tightened a faded purple sash around his waist. The sash held together a soiled shirt with no buttons. The only thing keeping the clothing in place was the sash. His footwear was strange too.

Leather straps encircled the man's calves up to his knees. The binding held the soles and hosiery in place.

"I'm James." He blushed at feeling as if he had to fill the air with more than the sounds of tools striking rock.

"Lok." The Chinaman removed his cone-shaped hat and ran his fingers through matted black hair. "You work more. I carry. No whip."

James nodded at Lok. He hurried with the work at hand to appease the nervous small man. In moments, James had loosened enough earth for Lok to shovel and fill buckets. Lok hefted the stick with the buckets swinging beneath his arms. Choppy footsteps carried the man into the darkness with another load for the sifters outside.

"I'm tired, James. When can we sleep?"

Carson slid down the wall and dropped his small pick into the detritus. James felt proud of his friend. The boy managed to come this far without collapsing. James understood Carson's plight as he had the same emotions.

"Soon, buddy. Soon." James lifted Carson back to his feet as the sound of Remus Phillip's voice echoed off the walls, getting louder as the man approached. "Get up and give it hell for a little longer."

Carson giggled at James' profanity. He pointed at James like he would tattle on him to Sarah.

James envisioned his mother's beautiful face and for the first time since they had left Texas, James really began to feel homesick.

Chapter Four

They had lost all sense of time down in the mine. While it felt as if they had worked the whole night through, James guessed Remus had cut them off around one in the morning. That would have meant the miners had been awake for twenty-four hours. Mr. Phillips had them start on the final leg of the journey at the same time the night before. The mules and men had hoofed with sporadic, brief rests until they had arrived in Orick at supper time. The men were forced to chew small rations while they set up camp and then went directly into the mine until quitting time.

When James pulled his feet from his boots, it felt as if his body temperature dropped nearly ten degrees. He exhaled, rubbing his sore toes and heels. Carson slumped into his sack, boots and hat still on like he had been shot down where he stood. James chuckled and implored Carson to strip out of his dirty clothing.

"You'll rest better without all that junk."

Carson scrunched his face and begrudgingly tossed his hat and boots to the foot of the tent. He complained he was hungry. James dug into his pack and rooted around until his fingers found the hard tack. He ripped a fibrous chunk and handed it to Carson, who wasted little time devouring the meat.

James rubbed his eyes with the backs of his hands to avoid getting more grit in his lids. He knew mining would be arduous work, much harder than sweeping up after drunks or horses but he had underestimated the toll the labor would take on his frame. James wondered how the older guys like Skunk had been able to deal with the rough workload if he struggled as a younger man.

"Can I have some more?"

"No. We have just enough to supplement what they feed us here. I don't want to run out before we get a chance to buy more supplies." James ignored Carson's scowl. He also knew Carson would have nightmares if he slept on a full belly. Better to keep his friend satisfied just enough to quiet the pangs.

"Lok talks funnied."

James chuckled. "Yeah. But don't say that in front of him. I don't want trouble."

Carson burped. He rolled onto his side and watched James as he stripped off his blue jeans and shirt. Another several degrees of heat escaped his skin and the feeling refreshed James.

"I want to go home, James."

Carson was not the only one. James sighed and kept a positive expression for Carson's benefit. "I know, buddy. Once we get some money in our pockets, we'll go somewhere else." James laid down. "This forest is amazing though, isn't it?"

"The trees are bigger than the whole world."

James nodded in agreement. He never imagined the size of the trees he had overheard the miners talking about on the trail. When they mentioned big trees, James figured the forest would be more expansive than anything they had seen before. Little did he imagine the enormity of the redwoods. Their size made the boys feel as if they had entered a fantasy world.

"We should knock off. Tomorrow will be another long day and we need the rest."

Carson rolled to his back and clicked his teeth together.

"I'm ascared of the monster too."

James tsked. "I told you before. There ain't no monsters here."

CHAPTER 4

"You said that with the Screeper and he was real."

It was hard to argue with Carson's logic. James wanted to put the issue to bed so he could fall asleep. James raised up on one elbow.

"What proof do you have that there is a monster? Hm? Did you see a monster?"

Carson shook his head.

"Did you hear a monster?"

Carson shook his head again. "No."

James laid down. "There you go. If you can't see it or hear it then it must not be there."

The tent fell silent for several moments.

"I felt it."

James dragged the back of his forearm across his brow. Part of him worried Carson conjured up tales to get his way so they would exit the mining company. What if Carson was right, James thought?

"Don't I always save you from the monsters? Hm? Have I ever let you get hurt?"

Carson nodded. "I got shotted. Stabbed. Kidnapped."

"Okay. Okay. Forget I asked." James cut off Carson's list of injuries. James meant he had never gotten Carson killed but the more he recalled their adventures, James had done little to protect Carson from harm. The poor kid had been hurt many times.

"Tomorrow, I will look around the camp and see if I can find the monster for you. And if I do, I promise I will kill it so you won't be scared."

Carson closed his eyes and settled into his sack. James figured the boy had bought his lie for the time being. He would try to draw Carson out in the morning and find the true meaning behind the boy's fears.

As James massaged his forearms and wrists, Carson drifted to sleep. The rhythmic, hushed snore signaled his friend had finally passed out from the intense schedule. James focused on his own breathing, attempting to slow his mind to the same speed of his body which had shut down minutes ago. Their adventures across the west had been exciting. And dangerous. However, James felt a stronger urge to settle down than he had ever known. Since childhood, his dreams had taken him along a heroic path in his father's footsteps. Over time, James realized the adventures were fun but he craved more routine. Not necessarily safety. Just a sense of being home.

Perhaps he could find a place they would like to be and fight the evil in that town. There had never been a shortage of bad guys passing through any place. Why travel so far from home in search of evil? When it was everywhere.

James yawned and licked his chapped lips with a tangy, dry tongue. Images of his mother and their farm in Texas played on a fuzzy stage in his mind as slumber pulled James into a world where his aching limbs no longer felt their pain.

Chapter Five

They had fallen asleep as soon as their heads touched the ground. James recalled the rhythmic snores from Carson's side of the tent as he fixated on the pole above. His limbs ached but the pain paled in comparison to the throbbing along his lower back. James awoke to pins and needles along his extremities. Sounds of the forest coming to life outside forced James to sit up and begin his day.

Carson remained fast asleep.

Several men began shouting and the peaceful dawn transformed into a chaotic commotion beyond the flimsy canvas of the tent. James hurried to shove his swollen feet into his boots. He stepped outside the shelter without his shirt, focused on the trouble ahead. As he neared the pack of onerous miners, several factions of men shoved each other in the center of the encampment.

A lanky man with missing teeth begged for help to search for his friend. His eyes brimmed with tears, panicked over his friend's disappearance.

"Quinn never came back. I tell you, it ain't like him. I looked everywhere but he's nowhere."

James spied the diminutive Lok on the periphery of the shoving match. "Who is Quinn?"

The Chinaman answered without taking his eyes from the upset miner. "He cook."

"You gonna cry over your woman or fix us some grub?" The main combatant pushed the lanky man backwards, pulling the circle of men forward with him.

James remained on the outside of the scuffle, avoiding the tussle. Ordinarily, James would feel compelled to get involved but he decided to pick his battles since they found themselves amongst strong, crazed men. The fight broke out into several smaller battles. Men paired off, throwing jabs and kicking bodies. One miner's nose bled profusely, turning the dusty soil into knotted clumps of dark crimson.

One faction of men only cared about filling their starving bellies with a hot breakfast, missing cook be damned. The others defended their missing friend and implored a search party be formed to locate their friend. James pieced together the story as the pugilists grumbled. Quinn had arisen early to gather wild mushrooms and redwood needles for fresh tea. But the man had gone missing. The cook's fire vacant of griddle and pots surprised the first men who made their way towards the chow line.

Skunk barged into the fray, wordlessly tossing men aside with one hand. He whirled two brawlers into the forest by the scruff of their collars. Stomping into the middle of the battlefield, Skunk glared at each man long enough to force their gaze downward in shame.

"Boss man will hand out lashes if you misbehave. Now, what the hell is going on here?"

The lanky man with few teeth dabbed at his bloodied lips with the back of his shirt sleeve before explaining how Quinn disappeared and nobody cared to help looking for him. Skunk listened with undivided attention, his intense eyes scouring the tree line for signs of treachery. When the other man interrupted to demand someone make his breakfast, Skunk strode directly at the man and squeezed his throat in a bear-sized paw. He pulled the reddened face close and gritted his teeth.

"I aim to get paid with or without you."

CHAPTER 5

Choking through the fist, the man twitched with lack of oxygen, his eyes wide with fear of never breathing again.

Skunk dropped the man to the dirt. He spun around and pointed at the miners. "The work is hard enough without us at each other's throats."

He spat and ran a hand through his wild mane of peppered hair.

"McConkey, Jesper and Toms. Come with me to look for Quinn."

"Hold up."

James shivered at the sudden voice which struck all the wrong nerves along his body.

Remus slid between some men and approached Skunk. He twirled the switch through his fingers.

"I suggest you fellas get to work. We still have to make up for lost time."

"What about Quinn?" Skunk spoke for his men.

Remus smirked. The lines along his green eyes drew his pale flesh towards his temples.

"No time will be wasted on deserters."

"The men said he went missing. He didn't walk away." Skunk maintained his position as spokesperson for the crew.

Remus chuckled. "Way I see it, one less mouth to feed means our profitability improved."

"We're hungry."

A brave soul shouted from the back of the crowd. Remus glared along the faces to find the person who dared to speak out.

"I'll whip up a modest snack to take the edge off. Until then, you men get down that hole and do what you are getting paid to do. Time is a wasting."

Disenchanted mumbling and groans resounded as the men dispersed to gather their tools and make haste to the mine. James turned to go awaken Carson when Remus stopped his progress with a soft hand in the center of his bare chest. James held Remus' gaze, afraid to back down from the tyrant.

"I hope your childish frame fills out soon. If it doesn't then I will know you ain't working hard enough."

Remus chewed the inside of his cheek as he grinned.

"Those who don't work hard get introduced to my lady." Remus tapped James' shoulder with his switch.

After a few awkward moments of silence, James continued to the tent to wake Carson. When he entered, Carson began to stir. James shook his head at his friend. He wished he could sleep through such a fracas like his little buddy. James felt thankful Carson got an extra few minutes of rest before the long day they had ahead of them. He knew ten or twelve hours of labor would be more than they can stomach after only a few hours the night before. James wondered if they could find a way to pace themselves so they could build up to the endurance of the men. His mind returned to the tiny Chinaman. If Lok could outwork the miners, then James and Carson would stand a chance to survive the workload.

Carson scratched the sleep from the corners of his eyes and yawned.

"Well, one of us can survive." James snickered aloud.

Carson, smiled with well-rested aplomb, oblivious of James' slight.

Chapter Six

The sound of iron connecting with stone drowned out the grunts of exertion along the mine shaft. Men toiled in silence for several hours as the callous reaction of the boss ruminated in the back of their minds. James figured the miners felt as he did. They were not human beings. Only flesh and blood mules for the mining company. The single-minded focus of the firm had been evident with an exclamation point.

James stole a glance at Carson. Dirt streaked the sweaty little face that strained with the heft of the tool in his small hands. Carson labored on, unaware that James stared at him. His tongue darted towards the corners of his mouth with each swing. First to the left. Then to the right. A perfect cadence with the swing of the hammer.

James smiled with pride at his friend.

Lok snapped his fingers at James. He startled at the realization he had been caught.

"You work more. I carry. No whip." Lok pointed at the wall.

"Yeah, yeah." James attacked the mine with renewed vigor.

Lok shoveled loosened soil into his buckets. He lifted the pole to his shoulders and hustled into the darkness with his payload. James watched after the small man as his form drifted from the cone of lantern light into the shadows. He wondered if carrying loads of buckets were easier than chipping at the walls all day long.

Carson complained his belly "hurted" without food. He lied and said they would have lunch within the hour. James hoped it would appease the boy's hunger pangs for a while. Lok soon returned, tightening his purple sash after lowering the empty buckets.

"How long have you been doing this, Lok?"

The small man straightened his cone-shaped straw hat and shook his head.

"Long time."

James dug into the rock. His shoulders ached and he felt the bicep muscle in his right arm begin to twitch.

"Do you like this work?"

Lok hocked some phlegm from the back of his throat and spat it into the darkness.

"No like work. No choice."

James lowered the pickaxe. "No choice? You can quit and do whatever you like."

Lok stifled a laugh into his palm. "YOU have choice. Lok have no choice. Country no like Chinese."

The Chinaman explained how he had been brought to America as a slave to pay off his father's debt in his homeland. He worked on railroads and in brothels. But his chances for survival had improved in the mines.

"White man whip Lok. Black man beat Lok. No trouble here."

Lok stabbed a finger at the wall to redirect James to chipping as he listened.

"Boss man leave alone. Work hard. Eat. Coin. No trouble."

He told James he wanted to save enough money so he could travel back to China to pay off his father's debt and return to his family's farm. He missed his wife and six children. James tried to imagine how Lok must feel having been torn from his homeland and loved ones. His own homesickness paled in comparison. At least he had Carson at his side. Lok had no one.

CHAPTER 6

James decided he would befriend Lok and act as his family away from home.

"We can help look out for you, Lok. Pretend Carson and I are your brothers."

Lok shook his head and spat again.

"Lok brother in China lazy like you. No need more brothers like you."

James rolled his eyes and smashed the axe into the rock. He would chip away at the small man's temperament like he chipped away at the gold ore.

Skunk appeared like a wraith from the shadows. His sudden presence startled James from the corner of his eye.

"Keep up the good work, boys."

Skunk stared down at Lok. "You standing guard or working?"

"I work. No whip. I carry."

Skunk laughed. The deep volume of his belly laugh rumbled along the walls.

"Relax son. I know you're one of the good ones." Skunk slapped Lok's shoulder so hard the Chinaman bounced off the wall. He squared up as if to fight off the larger man. "Save the aggression for the work or the wild man. I mean you no harm."

Skunk evaporated beyond the lantern light, deeper into the mine.

James remembered Skunk mentioning the wild man the previous day. With Carson complaining of a monster in the forest and notions of a wild man, James thought it an odd coincidence.

"Hey, Lok. What is a wild man? I keep hearing about him?"

Lok jammed his shovel into the floor and lifted the pole with all the buckets dangling from it. He grunted as he tucked the contraption behind his neck.

"White man stories. Scare men to work hard."

James mopped the sweat from his brow. The red callouses along his palm traced lines of dirt across his forehead. "So it is make believe?" He huffed and nodded down at Carson who paused to listen. "Told you there ain't no monsters."

Carson stuck his tongue out. James chuckled, pleased to have put the scare to bed with his little friend.

Lok stutter-stepped his way past them with his payload teetering across his shoulders.

"White man stupid."

James shrugged his shoulders. He couldn't argue with Lok but he felt men of all colors were stupid. That is how so much evil existed around the world. But James wanted to prove that one white man could make a difference. He swore to himself that he would skim some of their earnings and set it aside so Lok could return to China sooner than he dreamed possible.

Maybe fighting bad men was only part of the equation. Helping good men could be just as important as taking out the evil ones. James' brain worked through his newfound philosophy as he struggled to compete with the lactic acid that threatened to shut his limbs down. They had no means of telling time in the darkened mine but James estimated they had been working for three or four hours already and he wished they could take a break.

"My belly hurted again."

James felt his stomach groan with emptiness in sympathy with Carson.

"I'm hungry too, pal." He grimaced and swung the axe. "Me too."

Chapter Seven

As they exited the mine, the men squinted at the setting rays of sunshine capping the tops of the redwoods. Even from such a distance, the miners' eyes required adjustment to the brightness the tunnels lacked. Rumors swirled through the clumps of men while they headed back to the encampment. Quinn was still missing. No sign of the man existed. Not a drop of blood. No boot prints in the sandy soil. Not a fern leaf out of place.

Carson stuck close to James. He feared getting lost amongst the throng of miners. And the last thing he wanted was to be left alone for the monster to kidnap him. Carson glanced about, worried he would pick up the dangerous signals again. Luckily, the creature was not around. Carson's shoulders slouched after he realized he had them raised, knotted and full of tension.

James tried to whisper with the other men but he hadn't been quiet enough because Carson had heard it all. Something truly haunted the northwest. Many local Indian tribes described the beast who roamed the mountains and forests of the region. The Yurok called it "Omah." Karok Indians called the creature "Madukarahat" which loosely translated as "giant." The Shasta and Tulowa named it "Sasquatch." In the end, all the tribal lore described the wild man as an enormous beast, standing high above the tallest limbs. It was said to be covered in hair and resemble the countenance of a man.

Yet, it was feared by all.

The Sasquatch was known to steal babies in the middle of the night. They were said to feast upon human flesh. Many brave warriors had been torn apart, sinew from bone, in an effort to protect their tribes. Until one day when the bravest of warriors communed with the beast. An offering was made to ensure the survival of the species as well as protect the innocent children of the tribes. The Sasquatch would be respected and would no longer be hunted. In exchange, Sasquatch could have their fill of animal, whether horse, buffalo, or swine. And upon the harvest moon, one member of a given tribe would be sacrificed to the giants of the forest.

Carson whimpered to himself. His imagination went to darkened corners of his mind. He pictured the wild man storming through teepees with children squirming in his arms, and a bloody infant gushing from his fangs.

James forced a smile down at Carson. He turned his shoulder to eclipse more of the conversations.

After all the monsters they had encountered, Carson feared the wild man most of all. Somehow, in a forest where the trees stretched high into the clouds, the thought of an animal that was as tall horrified him. Regular beasts like bears and Chupacabra's, mountain lions and wild horses resembled pets compared to what his mind conjured of the wild man.

James held the tent flap open so Carson could crawl inside. A shiver tickled his loins and Carson realized he had to pee pee. He begged James to come with him behind the tent but James chastised him for acting like a baby.

"The sun is still out. You really think a monster is going to grab you with me inside the tent and all the men around camp?"

Carson nodded emphatically.

James groaned and slammed the flap down behind him. Carson listened as James grumbled to himself. Carson had little time to waste. He clutched at his crotch and wiggled his legs to stem the flow of urine. He had to relieve himself and the longer he waited, the quicker the sun would drop behind the crests, leaving him alone in the forest with his haunter.

CHAPTER 7

Carson bit his lip and tiptoed to the back of the tent. Staring along the undergrowth of lush fern leaves and shady redwood trunks, Carson searched for the eyes that would reveal the monster before him. Each shadow took on the shape of an enormous creature. Leaves waving in the gentle breeze tricked Carson into believing a head peeked around the trees. He shivered with another surge of urine and gave up holding it in. Carson undid his pants and freed himself to release a hard, steady stream of pee. The relief was instantaneous. He smiled as the leaves danced in his stream and went from dry pale green to wet darkness.

As his bladder emptied, Carson again sensed the thing which hid within the forest. His hair stood on end. The last drop of urine reversed course inside him to hide from what he felt was nearby. Carson's pants slid down his legs and gathered at his ankles.

His hands shook.

The shadows around the dense woods loomed and stretched down to taunt him.

Carson heard it. He couldn't see it.

I WON'T HURT YOU.

The trembling forced an extra squirt of urine to shoot upon the ferns.

Carson froze in place.

NOW IS NOT THE TIME. I WILL COME BACK. BE NOT AFRAID.

As suddenly as the sensation had hit him, the monster had gone away.

Carson turned to run back to the tent but tripped over his pants which tangled the bottom of his legs. Hyperventilating, Carson pulled himself to his feet and yanked his dungarees up to his waist. A cloud of mine dust billowed around him as he buttoned the pants and ran for the front of the tent.

James sat on his bag, kneading his toes and heels. Carson dove into his sack and pulled it over his head. He quietly cried to himself as James yelled at him to knock it off. Carson had to tell James all about his encounter but he didn't know how to explain what he couldn't see. It had been a feeling. And a strange voice in his head. He knew the voice was not his own because he had been too scared to even think about speaking let alone utter words.

Carson ignored James' pleas to follow him to the fire to get supper. James finally offered to bring something back for Carson but he knew he had no appetite. Food was unimportant when something horrific watched for him from the forest.

He tugged the blanket closer to his body, feeling his hot breath bounce back upon his face as he sobbed to himself.

Chapter Eight

The food was extra salty and dry. James knew without the camp cook at the helm, the meals would be overcooked and without flavor. Kidney beans in sauce, heated to crispiness and covered with charred venison did little to delight the taste buds. Where it lacked robust flavor, the meal made up for satisfying the hunger pangs of a long day of hard work.

Carson stomached a few bites before sliding the tin dish away from his sack. James had noticed the change in Carson's mood. Before supper, the boy had complained the monster had frightened him while he peed in the woods. James chalked it up to more childhood fantasies until he observed the boy's defeated body language. He wanted to draw his friend out without feeding the insanity of his nightmares.

"You need to eat more or you'll run out of energy tomorrow. Even if you aren't hungry, it is best to eat up."

Carson stared sullenly at the top of the tent. His arms cradled his head as he lie silent.

James tossed an errant bean that had jumped his plate. It bounced off Carson's nose and skittered into the corner of the tent.

"You should have paid attention." James mocked his little friend.

Carson remained stoic.

"Okay, what's the matter? Are you still sore about the monster scaring you out back?"

"It's not funnied, James. You never listen to me."

James sighed. He wriggled his sore feet and thought about rubbing them but gave up when he considered the effort it would require for him to bend forward and reach them.

"Come on. I listen to you all the time. Have you forgotten all the times I saved you?"

Carson rolled onto his side, exposing his back to James. As the boy grew older, James thought he became more difficult to deal with. When he was younger, James could manipulate Carson into anything by feeding his dreams or turning chores into adventures. Nowadays, Carson required more deft reasoning and logic to spur him into action.

"So tell me what it looks like? I'll need to know when I go kill it."

Carson snorted over his right shoulder. "Can't seed him."

"Well, then I go back to my original question. How do you know it is there if you can't see it?"

"I just know it. That's how."

James scrunched his nose. Carson's riddles drove him crazy. "You can't see it. You just know it's there." James shifted on his rump to face Carson more directly. "Describe how you know."

Carson turned over. His hands pleaded with James. "It talked to me. And I felt it staring at me. Remember when Sarah catched us when we broked the chair?"

James recalled the time his mother had known without any hint on earth that the boys had accidentally broken the kitchen chair before she had sat on it. She had come into the kitchen, glanced between the boys and then her attention went straight to the chair that set in the middle of the room. Sarah had asked what they had done and both boys slumped in admission of their guilt.

"So you just KNEW it was there." James mumbled his understanding.

"I said that already." Carson whined.

James crawled to Carson's side of the tent. He stretched his arm around his little friend.

CHAPTER 8

"I believe you, pal." James hugged Carson tight. "What did the monster say to you?"

Carson picked at dirt beneath his fingernails. He rolled grains of sand between his fingers before answering.

"It tolded me not to be ascared. And he wants me to wait until later."

"Wait until later?" James scratched his chin. He felt relief that the creature meant Carson no harm if it communicated as much. Unlikely Carson would conjure such a tale especially if he were so afraid of the monster. But what could it possibly mean asking Carson to wait for later? "What is gonna happen later?"

Carson shrugged. He bent to work on his filthy fingernails once more.

James preferred to seek the creature out rather than waiting for it to come back to Carson. James wished to take control. Besides, he could not risk losing Carson so James understood he would need to be much more vigilant about Carson always staying within sight.

"Do you think you can call it to us? I would like to see if it talks to me so I can figure out what will happen later."

Carson shook his head. "I don't know how to talk to it. I'm too ascared."

James rubbed Carson's back. He tried to imagine himself in Carson's boots. The world was much different from the boy's perspective. Youth and naivete collided with his disability, creating the most charming and vulnerable person.

"We can try though, right? Next time the monster talks to you, let me know and we will try to talk back this time. Sound like a plan?"

James smiled as Carson forced a nod that was more twitchy fear than agreement. James tucked Carson into his bag and kissed his forehead. Before James finished tucking himself in, Carson's breathing had fallen into a rhythmic tempo signaling he had drifted into dreamland. James thanked the Lord for Carson's peace. They needed to save their strength for the long day of labor ahead tomorrow. And for the battle that was coming. James knew in his gut that they had stumbled into the next set of troubles on their path for adventure. He had a similar premonition in their previous stops along the trail.

Visions of his mother feeding the farm animals in Texas took center stage in his mind. James allowed his lids to close so he could watch over his mother. His heart tingled with love and homesickness. James felt torn between continuing his journey to walk in his father's footsteps and turning heel for home. The last place he felt he belonged for longer than a minute.

As James gently snored, something huge crept along the tree line behind their tent. Even with great care, the heavy steps forced the earth beneath its great weight to rumble, rattling the bones of the slumbering miners.

Chapter Nine

James left Carson inside the tent so he could scoop up a few extra minutes of sleep. The camp was abuzz with activity. Miners in long underwear or fully dressed began huddling near the fire in the middle. James heard a solitary voice fluctuating between even discourse and raised levels of excitement. He squeezed his way closer, ignoring the grunts and dirty looks of his grizzled coworkers.

Remus Phillips had the floor. He slapped the switch into his palm as he spoke. Remus warned the men against doing whatever they chose. He related how Simpson and Mickey had chosen to pursue finding the cook and now they too were missing. James wondered who the men were, trying to determine which name better fit the lanky fella with the mouth void of teeth. He couldn't help considering Carson's tale of a monster. The story took on more credence now that two more men had disappeared.

"You are here to work, not explore. The next man who goes outside the confines of the camp will be dealt with accordingly. This is not a game. Gold is what we are after and if you want to be paid then you need to work."

His green eyes narrowed beneath the red, fuzzy eyebrows.

James stiffened when Remus targeted him.

Remus spoke without blinking.

"I will also offer a generous reward to any man who identifies those who choose to go their own way." He pronounced the word as REE-ward.

"Nobody gets paid if we can't finish the job. So it is in your best interests to keep tabs on your fellow man. Have I made myself clear?"

A cantankerous rumble of grunts echoed along the wall of miners huddled around the fire.

Remus slapped the switch along his leg and dismissed the men. Some returned to their tents to finish dressing while others lined up at the chuck box where breakfast was being served. Apples and jerky were on the menu and it would do little to satisfy the pangs of hunger before heading into the mine.

On his way back to the tent, James stopped to gawk at several men who had collapsed one of the tents. They dug through a few packs and fought over the clothing, knives and sundry items left behind by the missing men. The miners, like vultures, picked the bones clean, absorbing the leftovers with little care given to the human beings that once owned the items. James wondered how things would be handled if Simpson and Mickey came back. Would the men return their booty or would Simpson and Mickey work themselves into a lather trying to recoup their losses from the others? The miners were not a friendly lot and each man carried the appearance of saloon brawlers. Either way, there would be quite a row if the men decided to come back and search for their possessions.

Decided to come back?

James snorted to himself. If the rumor of the wild man was true, and if the missing men had been kidnapped by the monster, then the deciding had been done for them.

"Nature always reclaims what it owns."

The thunderous voice shook James from his thoughts.

Skunk stood a bit too close with his arms folded as he glared at the men who smiled at their new keepsakes.

"Man toils in the fields and the woods but it is only folly."

James blinked the sun from his eyes as he stared upwards into the fuzzy face of the big man.

"Nature?" James bristled at how stupid his voice had sounded.

Skunk slapped his shoulder. He snorted some snot and swallowed it down. "Good Lord gives us just enough rope to hang ourselves with. And if we don't get caught in our own noose then the soil devours us whole." Skunk winked. "You got religion, son?"

James believed in God and had been steadfast in attending services with his mother. Although, most of the attendance had been required by Sarah. He thought wisely about how to respond, afraid he would say the wrong thing and cause the gentle giant to dislike him.

"Sir." James croaked through his nod.

Skunk smiled, pleased with the response. "Best you heed His teachings and steer clear of most others." His thick finger indicated the miners who walked away with the things that had belonged to Simpson and Mickey. "Keep close watch on that little fella of yours. Stories say he takes a liking to young ones more so than men."

James gagged on his tongue. He could not believe that Skunk was talking about the wild man but he needed to confirm it. "He?"

Skunk kicked at a stone in front of his boot. "Same as what took Quinn and most likely Simpson and Mickey."

James waited a beat before prodding more. He hoped Skunk would reveal himself but the pause itched James' brain like a caterpillar that had snuck inside through his ear.

"So it's true? About the wild man?"

Skunk glanced about as if he wanted to be outside of earshot of someone who could listen in. "Truer than the blood in your veins. Seen him myself. Long ago, I took to a pretty squaw in the Karok tribe. Those folks made dolls and totems to appease the beast. I teased them regularly thinking it was just a figment of that funny stuff they always smoked around the fire. But they showed me. Called him in and I gave up the best pair of britches I ever owned."

James gaped, incredulous.

"Only reason I admit this is because I have a strange feeling about these guys going missing. We're too far away for a man or two to take off on their own without horses or supplies. Any man with half a mind would know their chances of survival in these parts would be small. Mountain men or Indians? Yeah, they'd be fine. But miners? No chance in Hell they would last longer than a day or two. So why would they risk it?"

James hazarded a guess. "The owner's son could probably chase some men away."

Skunk bellowed with laughter. He ran his fingers through his beard as his mirth subsided.

"No doubt but even that son of a devil is to be feared less than what's out there."

"So you believe in the wild man and you're not scared?"

"I respect him." Skunk cracked his knuckles before jamming his fists in his pockets. "Respect is stronger than fear. And he knows it." Skunk angled to leave James behind. "He only harms those who disrespect him and his home."

James burned holes into Skunk's back as he tried to process the unlikely source of all his questions. And fears.

Chapter Ten

James chose to keep Carson in the dark about his monster. The morning blew by in a flash once the work got underway. Carson picked, James axed and Lok hauled. A finely tuned machine, the trio performed their tasks in silence. Only their breath and tools made a sound.

The boys had gotten better in terms of their stamina and workflow. It had taken a few days for the body to adjust to the steady burden. And the picking became so predictable and repetitive to allow the mind to continue without focusing on the aches in the shoulders or the blisters on the hands.

Throughout the day, James attempted to engage Lok in more conversation. James had been careful to not break stride in his labor as he spoke, avoiding Lok's admonishing the possibility of getting whipped. Yet, Lok would refrain from engagement or would respond in one-word answers to cut off the discussion before it could get too lengthy.

Lok filled the buckets to overflowing and strained to lift the pay load to his shoulders. James threw down his pickaxe and hurried to assist the Chinaman. When he hoisted the pole up for Lok to slide under it, James whistled aloud, surprised at how heavy it was. He quickly respected the little man's strength. Something so heavy would require the force of two men in a normal situation but the small guy had managed it alone day after day - all day long.

The Chinaman mumbled what James interpreted as thanks in his native tongue before shuffling forward. As soon as Lok moved, James realized his tool lie across the path the man would travel. James shouted a warning and Lok twisted to glare at James for shocking him. In doing so, Lok lost balance and teetered to the left, juggling the spilling buckets to catch himself.

Lok's ankle twisted and rolled under.

Buckets and body crashed into the mine wall before smacking into the dirt. Lok groaned in anguish, clutching his lower leg. James and Carson rushed to his aid and began freeing the way for Lok to sit up.

"Oh no. Hurt now."

Carson giggled at the pidgin English. James shot Carson a look that went unnoticed.

"Let me see it." James gently clasped Lok's foot and his fingers searched along the flesh beneath to find any signs of fracture. The bones were intact but Lok's flesh swelled to a size that resembled a thigh more than a calf. Lok winced and rocked on his buttocks.

James let go. "It's a nasty sprain but I don't think anything is broken."

"Lok whipped. Big trouble."

A heavy stride resounded along the walls as the man with the bite taken out of his felt hat came into view. James waved the man over. "Stumpy."

"The name is Dusty. What's going on here?"

James bit his lip for forgetting the man's name. "Twisted ankle. Can you help me carry him out?"

Dusty shook his head and raised his hat back to get a better look. A closer inspection elicited a clucking of his tongue. "Can't carry him out. He'll be whipped and shot for wasting our time."

"Shot?" James barked in disbelief. "What for?"

Dusty stood up. "Chinks ain't worth a penny if they can't work. Boss man would just as well put him down as keep him on as a liability."

"His ankle will heal. Lok will be good as new in a few days."

CHAPTER 10

Dusty chuckled. "I wish it were different, boy. His kind ain't got no rights in this country. They're like cattle. Bought and sold and used up. Once he ain't no good then there is no need to care for him."

James panicked. How could he let the man be killed when he had promised himself to help pay the man's way back to his homeland?

"What if I trade jobs with him? Lok can keep his weight off his foot while he strikes the rocks and I will carry the buckets up and down?"

Lok darted his eyes between James and Dusty. Dusty scratched at his butt as he considered James' suggestion.

"Well, I suppose that would work. Boss man might question why you are the one going back and forth instead of the Chink." He tilted his head from side to side. "But the work would keep getting done so it wouldn't warrant any drastic measures."

"Great." James helped Lok to his good foot and leaned him against the wall. He handed Lok his pickaxe and hurried to shovel the loosened stones into the buckets.

Dusty nodded and wished them luck. He disappeared in a cloud of filth and shadows.

"You help Lok."

James saw the water grow to spilling within Lok's eyes. He nodded at the smaller man. "We're friends. Friends help each other, right?"

Lok's lower lip quivered. "Friends."

James nodded again and lifted the heavy pay load onto his shoulders. He felt the burden light fires within his thighs and once more James wondered how the smaller man had been able to work so hard for so long with less size.

"Carson, keep an eye on Lok in case he loses balance."

Carson made a circle with his thumb and forefinger that he got it.

"And Lok, do me a favor. Make sure nobody hassles Carson. He's just a boy."

Lok smiled out of one side of his mouth. James left the pair behind as he navigated between well-lit sections of tunnel and parts where the darkness enveloped him to the point where even the sound of axes quieted to a level of nonexistence. James trained his eyes on the faint glow of the next lantern ahead. He adopted Lok's method of flat-footed shuffling to ensure his path was straight and clear. With another disaster averted, James began to work the details on how to bring the wild man closer so he could assess Carson's safety. If the creature spoke to Carson and told him it was coming back then James would have to deal with the beast head on.

For good or for worse.

Chapter Eleven

Remus Phillips glowered at James each time he dumped the buckets into the sifters. James diverted his attention to stay out of the man's cross hairs. But he knew it would only be a matter of time before his confrontation came to fruition.

James paused to check on Lok and Carson when inside the mine. Ever since the swap in tasks had occurred, Lok had loosened up. He became more chatty, which James understood to be hardly chatty at all in the normal world. For Lok, it had been downright verbose. Carson also came out of his shell. Since joining the mining company, Carson had been quiet or frozen in fear. With Lok in their companionship, the trio had formed a family dynamic which eased the tensions of the daily labor.

As the afternoon drew on, James noted how Remus slowly moved closer to the sifter where he unloaded. He felt the tension knot his shoulders, expecting the inevitable. James lowered the pole and began dumping buckets into the sifter. Remus Phillips sauntered with calculated steps, intimidating and positioned in power.

The switch met his forearms, impeding his progress of emptying the next bucket.

"I see you have been busy delivering ore."

James ignored the wise crack that threatened to escape his lips. "Yes, sir."

Remus circled James. He felt the beady green eyes dissecting his soul from behind. Remus rounded into view again and paused.

"Where's the kid?"

"My brother is in the mine. Working hard." James controlled the hostility in his tone.

"You know, our company has a hard line against child labor." Remus tapped his palm. "But my father agreed to your terms. Two for the price of one."

James bristled. The agreement wasn't quite a two for one trade in labor. It was agreed upon that Carson would earn half a man's wages since it was expected he would only be capable of doing the work of half a man. James made a mental note to reconfirm the terms of their employment at a more opportune moment.

"It would behoove you to keep a closer eye on your kin. A mining outfit can be a dangerous place for a youngster."

James looked at the buckets at his feet. He wanted to dump them quickly and get back into the mine but he worried Remus would find it disrespectful to carry on without giving the boss his undivided attention.

"Did you know that in China, little boys are used as FREE labor? And the ones who lack skills for the fields are used for more intimate pursuits."

James clenched his fists. Remus' insinuation was meant to provoke him.

"Knowing such information, I might think twice before I turned my back on a Chink with such tender flesh nearby. In a dark secluded tunnel with a difficult means of escape."

James stepped into Remus' personal space. He jutted his face close enough to smell the tobacco which lingered along the man's skin. "Some people might think twice before causing a man to act on his principles."

Remus smirked. He closed the gap between them, pressing the tip of his nose against James'. The sign was clear. Remus would not back down nor would he be dissuaded from his repulsive behavior. "Ready when you are, Mr. Johnson."

A small crowd had begun to form as the scent of blood in the air drew the buzzards. The miners kept silent to get an earful of every word. The men ate up fights. And a fight between a laborer and a boss would fetch the greatest attention.

"Can I get back to work? Sir?" James spat the last word so Remus would have to wipe his chin clean of saliva.

"Hey."

The miners shifted to the side as the newcomer broke the stare down. Of course, neither James nor Remus shifted their attention away from the other.

Skunk stomped into the sphere of hostility. Dusty was close behind.

"Is there a problem, Mr. Phillips?"

"None whatsoever. We were just discussing the protection of Mr. Johnson's brother."

"The boy is fine. I just saw him a few moments ago." Dusty pointed back at the tunnel in the hill.

Remus tore his gaze from James. "Did you authorize the change in assignments?" Remus addressed Skunk. Skunk looked quizzically at James.

"I volunteered to carry the buckets down for Lok." James interjected before Skunk could stammer on an answer.

"You just felt compelled to change roles and do whatever you please? Hm?"

Dusty stepped forward. "The Chink twisted his ankle and he thought it better to help out rather than losing the Chink's hands."

Remus raised his switch high above his head. The sudden motion forced a collective gasp from the onlookers. He slowly lowered his arm as if he had only been stretching his shoulder.

"I appreciate your fastidious decision to save the company money. However, all direction or duties and responsibilities can only be dictated by myself or Skunk. Is this understood, Mr. Johnson?"

"Yes, sir." James allowed his breathing to normalize for a moment.

"Perhaps you should get back to your brother before he becomes Lok's concubine."

James began to step into Remus when Skunk's massive bicep held him in place.

"You heard the boss. Get back to work." Skunk spun around. "All of you."

The crowd quickly dispersed. Grumblings of disappointment for no bloodshed could be overheard. James listened to Skunk, picked up his pole and buckets and trudged up the slope to enter the mine shaft. Remus stared after James.

"He's a good kid. Works his tail off." Dusty offered his assessment as he walked away.

"Any man who stands up for an immigrant cannot be trusted." Remus turned on Skunk. He jammed the switch into the larger man's chest.

The switch bent as if it met solid stone.

"Keep your eyes on that man. If he or that Chink step out of line once...I want to hear of it. Am I clear?"

Skunk nodded. "Clear, sir. I will personally see to it myself that they toe the company line."

"Very good. Why can't all employees be like you?" Remus meant the question as rhetorical. He drifted back up the line of sifters toward the section that sat under the shade of the trees.

"All your employees are just like me. They hate your guts too."

Skunk muttered and strode back to the mine.

Chapter Twelve

The camp went completely dark once the fire burned out. A swatch of orange glowing embers remained where the flames had consumed all the kindling. Raucous snores intermingled with the insects in the forest floor. Another day of mining activity in the books and one day closer to yielding the biggest gold product uncovered in northern California.

The crickets ceased their chatter.

A soft mountain breeze went to ground as the world's safety came into question. Even the cirrus clouds passing the moon's glow evaporated in a final effort to hide from the danger that lurked.

The ground rumbled.

On the east side of camp, the earth trembled in a growing crescendo. A train barreling into town where no tracks were set.

Thunder cracked above in limbs bigger than rail cars as they rained to the forest floor. Men in sheer terror shouted from under their bags. A few miners who gave into their fears, scrambled from their tents, and ran for the safety of the trees.

The ground bounced as several beasts as big as the redwood trees stormed through the camp. The chuck box splintered into thousands of pieces. Mules dropped in place with crushed skulls and gore exploding from warm bellies.

One miner ran for the tunnel but never reached his haven of safety as he flattened beneath the hefty stomp of a wild man. Roars loud enough to vibrate the souls of man caused bladders to empty and bowels to void.

Carson cried aloud. James held him tight and listened to the horrific sounds outside the thin layer of tent fabric. He first thought the camp had fallen under attack of a tribe of Indian warriors. Then he wondered if a massive storm had moved into the mountains, sending an avalanche of snow and wood hurtling towards them. But the screams had brought James back to reality. He knew from the terror-inducing bellows that something more monstrous had come to visit.

The wild man.

He clutched Carson with one arm and felt along the tent floor with his other arm, desperate to find his pistol or knife. James recalled they had been stowed at the bottom of his pack to keep them safe from thieves' hands. He would never retrieve the weapons without leaving Carson alone. And Carson shook uncontrollably against his chest.

"I'll be right back."

"No, James." Carson hollered, barely audible above the din.

"Is it talking to you?"

Carson shook his head but James wasn't sure if it was in response to his question or further evidence of his fear.

"Carson, I have to go out there. Our only chance is to get out of here but I need to find the quickest way to get into the woods without being discovered."

"No, James."

Ignoring his friend, James used all his might to peel Carson's fingers from his limbs. He dug into the bottom of his pack, tucked his hunting knife into his boot and strapped his holster around his waist. Out of habit, James spun the cylinder to ensure each chamber had been filled with lead. In the darkness it was a useless use of time.

CHAPTER 12

"Don't go anywhere." James instructed Carson whose cries rose to an irritating pitch. He stepped outside and observed an absolute scene of destruction. Men ran back and forth. Tents lie flat. The sound of levered action rifles pumping cartridges before the spark of being fired taunted him from every direction. James stared beyond the back of their tent which had purposely been situated closer to the tree line to keep them away from the miners. The darkness of the woods enveloped his field of vision.

Something moved in that darkness. James narrowed his lids to slits, focusing all his vision at the shadow which appeared blacker than the void around it. It moved closer. Slow. Steady.

Massive.

James pulled his six shooter from his hip. He lifted it straight out, unsure of how small to aim as the movement could have been the size of a mountain. Then it stepped forward. James, stunned at what stood before him, dropped his arm to his side.

The face of a man, hidden in the foliage of dark hair from head to toe, glared down at him. James felt like wetting himself but he caught the release just in time.

"Are you," James started to ask what he needed to know but his voice vanished.

A gaping mouth as wide as a man is long, stretched across thin lips, revealing a mouth full of enormous white teeth. Oddly, none of the teeth looked sharp. No fangs. Just square teeth like he and Carson had.

A whoop from the far side of camp distracted the wild man in front of him. It crunched root and rock along its path to join its brethren in the destruction of the mining camp. James remained frozen in place for what felt like hours but could only be seconds. He followed the sounds of gun fire and monstrous screams. He stumbled over bodies torn in half and appendages that no longer belonged to a host. James swallowed back his bile and raced to the aid of the men. As he sprinted James questioned if he should join the fray and risk the monsters' ire. He'd be better off saving

Carson. But fighting off the beasts would be a way to save Carson too. And fighting was more in line with James' instincts.

As he left Carson behind, something massive moved toward their tent. It breathed like it had lungs as large as iron-burning cauldrons. Each breath so strong it forced the tent flaps to wave as if caught in a summer storm. The wild man who had spoken to Carson knew the boy waited inside. It needed the boy. And now there was nothing between its desires and the human who cowered below. The monster lifted the tent with two fingers like it were a sock on a laundry line. It cast the fabric aside and leaned down, nearer the object of its needs. The monster sniffed at the ammonia smell of urine surrounding the small, trembling frame.

"No." A small whimper sounded from under a thin layer of bag which could not deny the creature.

Chapter Thirteen

Carson's body flopped loosely under the wild man's arm. His legs scraped along tree trunks as the creature carried him deeper within the forest. Not that Carson felt a thing. His mind gave up all thoughts and reason once the monster had scooped him up.

After several minutes of floating beneath the canopy of the ether, Carson became aware of his surroundings. The first thing he felt was the rush of foliage breezing through his hair. It was refreshing against his exposed skin which had been flushed and burning hot with stress. Carson then noticed the stench which assaulted his nostrils. Akin to an outhouse in the noon-day heat and a sweaty cowpoke who had not bathed along the trail, Carson's eyes watered. He attempted to clasp a hand over his face to ward off the odor but his arms were locked under the clutch of the beast's armpit. Long, wispy hairs dangling from the monster's arm brushed along Carson's face, tickling his nose and cheek.

In the distance, a horrific roar shook the forest, seemingly coming from everywhere at once. The wild man who carried him growled a deep guttural response. The noise vibrated every organ in Carson's body. He felt a rush of urine escape and warm his dungarees. Carson tried to scream for help but the only thing that made it past his lips was a soundless breath. His lungs had no room to expand or provide the energy to shout for help.

Sensing his recovery, the wild man swung Carson across its chest from the right arm and tucked him just as tightly under its left arm. Carson gasped at the height of his precarious position. Even in the utter darkness, Carson made out the enormous space beneath himself to the ground. He caught a brief glimpse of the trail ahead where the monster carried him and the view reminded him of standing perched on a high cliff. Higher than the limbs Carson enjoyed climbing, the forest took on a whole different perspective, like a corridor in the clouds.

It grumbled again, trudging and stomping its way through the undergrowth. Sharp snaps of branches that stood in the way and succumbed to the path of the beast cracked all around them. Carson began kicking his legs and wriggling his arms, doing whatever he could to get away from the grasp of the wild man. The grip loosened for a moment before tightening so hard it squeezed a puff of gas from Carson's backside. Carson regained his voice and screamed with all his might. His pleas were quickly drowned out by the monster's roar. Another wild man directly ahead answered the roar with three, high-pitched whoops. To the left and right of the trail, woody knocks on trunks and what could have been rocks being clacked together signaled more of the beast's comrades in the area.

A break in the forest opened and the moonlight radiated like a newly lit lantern. The ground flattened across a huge patch of moss and needles. The softer ground resonated up the beast's legs and provided some shock absorption for Carson's flopping frame. In the center of the opening, two creatures hulked with excitement as if their heavy breathing forced their shoulders up and down at a frenetic pace. Carson wondered where their necks were as the massive heads seemed to grow straight out of their shoulders.

The monster carrying him stopped before the two who awaited. It swung Carson by his ankle, showing him off to the others like a fisherman holding his trout for his friends to appraise his catch. The motion nauseated Carson because he lost all sense of direction and his brain rattled around inside his skull. He felt the organ slosh and smack against bone.

CHAPTER 13

The creatures spoke in a dialect which Carson could not understand. The noise reminded him of Lok's speech when the man got frustrated and mumbled under his breath. But it also sounded like wood blocks or rocks punctuating at intervals. Clicks and pops tossed in the middle of gibberish. One of the creatures sounded like a youngster. The voice a tad softer and gentler. The second beast sounded masculine but not as deep as the one who had snatched Carson. He knew the one who held him aloft was the daddy or the leader. The confidence and dominance evident in its body language and words. It sounded like a boss giving orders to its workers. Carson trembled as he imagined how he would feel if he were the two who had awaited in the clearing.

The trio broke apart and scrambled in opposite directions. The one who Carson assumed was younger threw its arms high in the air towards a nearby redwood. In a smooth fluid motion, its legs wrapped around the girth of the trunk and the monster scrambled up the tree with an ease like a fish gliding down a brook. Before he could blink, the hairy man monster had disappeared far into the canopy. The second beast bounded into the tree line in three short steps, covering a wide space which resembled their farm in Texas. Carson mouthed his surprise at such quickness.

As the monster continued forward, it slung Carson's tiny frame back under its arm. Carson's nose wrinkled as the stench once again pummeled his senses.

"Let me go."

Carson shouted and the sound of his voice scared himself. He had no idea that he had recovered his instincts to defend himself. Once the realization alerted him, Carson used all his strength to scratch and kick against the monster. Each strike hurt him as if he had punched a brick wall or stone edifice. The pain seared his knuckles but did little to deter him from fighting harder. Carson had tried all he knew until he decided to sink his teeth into the monster's side. His mouth filled with sweaty hair and foul stench. Carson bit down and tasted an oily copper flood his tongue. The wild man howled. It struck a nearby redwood with a hammer fist and the tree splintered like an axe had come down on a stack of firewood.

Carson found himself falling, tumbling from the sky, and rushing towards the knotted, root-covered forest floor.

Chapter Fourteen

Remus Phillips cussed and shoved two men who stood shaking and dazed. He swung his switch as a follow up to the hand violence. The whip connected with both men, eliciting cries of anguish. Skunk rushed in to guide the injured men out of reach. Remus brought the switch back past his shoulder like a viper about to strike. He thought better of carrying out the corporal punishment on his foreman.

"Set up a perimeter. I want rifles at cardinal points at all times."

Skunk pointed at several miners who he had known to be handy with their Remingtons.

The destruction was catastrophic, even in the flickering fire light. Dusty dragged two bodies, torn to shreds and bloodied beyond recognition. He piled them next to a small stack of deceased that had already been collected.

James hurried to Skunk. He had searched everywhere for Carson but the boy was nowhere to be found. His innards roiled and threatened to force his last meal to make a splash on the outside.

"He's gone. Carson's gone."

Skunk's face scrunched. "Sorry, son. He was a good kid."

James shook his head and waved his hands. "No, not gone as in dead. Gone as in missing."

Dusty sidled up to Skunk's right. He swiped his brow with the back of his hand.

"Did you check under the tents? I found a few men that were crushed into the dirt."

Skunk held up a giant paw to keep Dusty from further upsetting James with gruesome imagery.

"Yes, yes. I looked everywhere. He's not here at all. I need to find him right away."

"You ain't going nowhere." Remus strode into the conversation with a purpose. He jabbed his switch into James' chest. "You're going to get to work like everyone else. First, you're going to bury the dead and then you're going to mine."

"I'm going after Carson." James swiped the switch away from his body.

"The boy's gone." Remus gritted his teeth. "The sooner you get that through your head, the better off you'll feel. Now get to work before I give you a beating you'll wish you were too dead to experience."

James pushed Remus over. The man stumbled backwards and fell to his back. His whip flew several yards away. Skunk wrapped his bear-sized arms around James and swung him out of Remus' reach. Dusty rushed to interfere with Remus who hopped to his boots and made to charge James.

"You'll die before you leave this camp, boy."

"I'm not afraid of you. I have battled much worse than your kind." James poked his finger in Remus' direction. His mind told him to hush up and find Carson, which was more a priority than exacting revenge on the boss man.

"Tie him up. Now. He'll get lashes and then we will try him once the dust settles on this mess." Remus failed to slough the grip of Dusty. His eyes widened with crazed aggression.

Skunk pulled James away, locking his arms under James' so he could do little to escape.

"What are you doing? Let me go. I gotta find Carson."

"Sorry, son. As much as I want to help you, I need to keep the order around here before we have a riot on our hands." Skunk dragged James whose boot heels carved a trail in the earth.

Remus rounded Dusty. He retrieved his whip and aimed it at James as he was pulled farther away.

"We ain't done here, Mr. Johnson. This has just begun."

Remus spat and slapped his switch against his thigh. He turned and shoved Dusty but the motion didn't affect the huge man's balance. Dusty shook his head and turned to help gather more bodies and fix up the camp.

James slumped against a redwood. He felt the smooth bark push into his spine. James squirmed against the solo fist that pinned him to the tree. With his free hand, Skunk tugged on the tent rope of a nearby destroyed hut. He chewed the twine from the canvas and deftly wound the rope around the tree, James and looped it through a knotted root which jutted from under James' legs.

"You can't do this. What about Carson? He's just a boy. I must find him. Please. Don't do this to me."

Skunk secured the rope with several knots which could lash a herd of cattle to a single post.

"Settle down for a bit and we will figure this out. Right now I need to calm the men down and get us back on track before boss man gives us all the lashes."

James felt tears well up and cloud his vision. He refused to cry in front of Skunk or any other man but the frustration overwhelmed his self-control.

"If anything happens to Carson I will die. Do you understand me? He is all I got and I swore I would always take care of him." James fought uselessly against his bindings. "Just let me go and I won't return. I promise. You can tell Remus you tied me up but I must have escaped somehow."

Skunk shook his head. "If you escape, boss man will know I didn't do my job and then I get the switch. If I get the switch...I don't know what I would be capable of doing next. But it would not be good. For me or for Remus."

"Please. Please." James begged as Skunk walked back to the middle of what used to serve as the miner encampment. With each step, James saw his hope fade into the darkness which remained of the night. He squeezed his eyelids tight, forcing the tears to run down his face. James imagined Carson, crying and scared, lost in the dense woods and praying for James to come rescue him.

The next scene which filled his mind shook James down to the marrow in his bones.

He saw Carson, ripped into pieces, scattered along the forest floor. Bones jutting from flesh and blood spatter on the ferns.

At the end of the trail, a humongous monster fed on the meat which had previously served as his little friend's body. The monster grinned and chewed, snapping a fragment of bone in its teeth before swallowing the boy whole.

Chapter Fifteen

BE STILL. YOU ARE SAFE.

Carson shivered as goose bumps puckered his skin. The monster spoke inside his head again. He scoured the den for an opening, hoping to crawl away and return to camp. His belly rumbled with hunger but Carson busied himself with plans of escape instead.

YOU WILL NEVER FIND YOUR WAY.

Carson blinked. The creature read his thoughts and spoke to him again. He wished he could read the monster's mind to find out how long he had left to live before it ate him.

The wild man made a sound which Carson interpreted as laughter.

His eyes adjusted to the darkened space. Carson could tell they were underground as sporadic root systems and patties of earth hung from above. A clump of long recesses filtered sunlight from above onto the earthen floor between he and the monster.

Carson's belly rumbled and he clutched at his midsection to quiet it down.

A long, hairy arm reached across the dappled light. Interspersed within the patches of long black hair, a grayish pale skin, coarse like leather, filled in the gaps. Thick black fingers unfurled revealing a dark fleshy palm. Tucked in the meaty hand were several plump figs.

Carson salivated and paused before taking the food. He feared the monster would grab his tiny hand and rip his arm out. But a peaceful wave passed over him. Carson thought he would have been devoured already if the creature had meant to eat him.

Tentatively and with measured care, Carson leaned closer and plucked one fig from the creature's hand. His arm retracted as if he tried to clear his flesh of a bear trap. However, the hairy arm had not flinched. Instead, it gently placed the remaining figs on the ground at Carson's feet. With ravenous abandon, Carson shoved the meat of the fig into his mouth. The juicy tender flesh erupted, coating his tongue, and dripping from his lips to his chin. Carson nearly swallowed the offering without chewing. He lifted a second one and ate heartily again.

Chewing sloppily, Carson decided to attempt communicating. He had many questions. So many thoughts it nearly ruptured his brain. What are you? Why did you take me? Where are we? Where is James?

The monster snorted and bent towards Carson. For the first time, he saw the face of the monster and the result was shocking. Black eyes buried under a roughened brow inspected him. Leathery black flesh wrinkled across the forehead as the creature concentrated on his face. A mouth wider than a horse, with thin brown lips stretched from one side of the massive skull to the other. Carson imagined a mouth large enough to bite the head off a buffalo in one try. Its nose appeared flattened like a saloon brawler but the nostrils flared wide, like two chocolate oh's big enough to fill lungs larger than lakes. Every inch of skin was covered in hair except for the nose and small stripe beneath the creature's eyes.

The shock came from the overall package. Carson thought it was a monster yet it looked...human. If Carson didn't know any better, he would swear he stared into the face of a man. A large, hairy man.

I AM NOT LIKE YOU.

Carson flinched at the sudden voice in his head.

YOU ARE SPECIAL. NOT LIKE THE REST.

CHAPTER 15

The words thundered in his skull. The sharp tone made his head ache but the mood behind the words felt soothing in a way. Carson rubbed at his temples.

YOU SMELL DIFFERENT. INNOCENT. WHOLESOME.

Carson understood little of what the monster said. He thought of James and wished he were close so he could explain what was happening.

JAMES IS NOT KNOWN. BUT YOU FEEL FOR IT.

Carson giggled. He slapped his fingers over his lips to stifle the laugh. It was funny how the monster called James an "it."

HIM.

It had read his mind and corrected itself.

WHAT IS THE NATURE OF JAMES?

Carson tilted his head as he absorbed more of the monster's appearance. He followed the face down to the muscular chest and rippled stomach flesh which shined through patches of hair.

FRIEND AND BROTHER. WHICH ONE?

"Both." Carson responded with his words. "I love him and I miss him."

The creature stroked Carson's cheek with a rough fingertip. It traced his nose and mouth before gently jabbing his pointy chin.

YOU ARE PURE OF HEART AND SOUL. NEVER HAVE WE ENCOUNTERED THIS BEFORE EXCEPT IN BABIES. BUT YOU ARE NO BABY.

Carson nodded. "I'm not a baby." He folded his arms across his chest and grimaced.

DO YOU TRUST ME?

Fidgeting with some dirt at the tip of his boot, Carson shrugged his shoulders.

YOU MUST KNOW IF I MEANT YOU HARM YOU WOULD BE NO MORE BY NOW.

Carson mumbled under his breath that he understood that.

I MUST SHOW YOU SO MUCH. WE MUST GO. NOW.

Carson popped the last fig into his mouth. He chewed quickly, swallowing the juicy innards before spitting the pulp into the side of the earthen wall. He rolled onto his knees and realized the ceiling of dirt overhead was too low for him to stand and walk. Then it dawned on him that the enormous creature before him would never be able to fit in such a confined space. Yet, there it was. Seated in front of him in the same cave. Carson began to question how it fit inside the cavern when the world blackened at the corners of his vision.

Rhythmic breathing steadied the boy as the monster scooped him up and began to work its way through a winding tunnel beneath the surface of the ground above. It sang a calming hymn into Carson's brain to keep him in deep slumber as they traveled. No human could know where they lived. For the safety of the clan, it forced Carson to a state of unconsciousness so he could never lead men back to where they stayed. Humans were dangerous and only meant harm to soil and beast. Even an innocent such as the boy could inadvertently reveal what must remain unknown for centuries to come.

As it had remained secret for centuries before.

Chapter Sixteen

Daylight cast a somber portrait of the devastation. Fragments of gear and remnants of clothing, some still clinging to a piece of its former inhabitant, littered the compound. Most of the detritus had been cleared before morning. The fire burned red hot in the center of the camp. Anything no longer useful was tossed into the pit and transformed into ember and smoke. Once they had a real body count, Remus ordered the dead to be laid in the fire as well. He said if they were going to spend time digging then it would be more fortuitous to do so down in the mines. Nobody cared to argue the nature of sacrilege of bypassing proper burials. To a man, the miners wanted to be done with the clean up and get inside the tight confines of the shaft where they would feel safer.

Everyone was spooked.

All told, nearly one third of the mining company had perished in the sneak attack of the previous evening. Remus outwardly complained more about the damaged tools and dead mules than the human beings who had succumbed to their injuries. His only worry was his family's bottom line. It seemed the only man Remus Phillips feared was his daddy. Rumor had it that his twin brother Romulus was far more evil than he. But Remus spoke of his brother's "office body" as an albatross on the family business. Romulus had graduated from stern field boss to financier and accountant back in the town where the company had opened its doors. Remus had been promoted to field general and had never turned back - cutting and slashing his way through ground, man and beast until the profits soared and daddy's approval came in the form of absentee leadership.

Skunk had tried to tone down the boss' vitriol to stem the tide of a mutiny. His words fell on deaf ears and luckily the men licked their wounds and carried on, happy to be alive and under the protection of a large company of men instead of being left to their own devices in the foreign and scary woods of northern California.

James had exhausted himself attempting to shed his bindings. He fell asleep in an awkward position and awoke to pins and needles all along his extremities. James whistled to grab Lok's attention and after several failed attempts, Lok slinked back to the tree line to greet his new friend.

"Help me outta this stuff."

Lok shook his head and glanced about nervously.

"Scared. No whip. No trouble."

James sighed. "Didn't I save you from Remus when you hurt your leg? Don't friends help one another?"

Lok made himself as small as possible, partly tucked into the foliage surrounding the tree.

The Chinaman shrugged but nodded.

"Lok come back. Lok help later."

"I might not be alive later, Lok. You gotta get me outta here now." James wriggled and expanded his chest to loosen the rope with little effect.

"Lok come back. You see."

"Dammit, Lok. Cut my bindings quickly and then you can run back to the group. Once they go down the mine I will be left alone. If Remus doesn't kill me without witnesses, then the thing that wrecked our camp will come back and eat me alive."

Lok nodded and sheepishly pulled a small knife from his laced-up shoe-sock. He worked the blade back and forth in short strokes, shredding the binding thread by thread. Once the knife broke through the last strand, James felt immediate relief wash across his chest and ribs. He hurried his

CHAPTER 16

hands to slip his legs free and then posed himself against the redwood so he was locked in place from a distance.

"Thank you, Lok." James rubbed life into his limbs. "Now hurry back and keep your head down. Signal me if you hear Remus coming for my throat."

"Lok no signal."

James groaned. He ran through different critter sounds he and Carson used to mimic when they hid in their forts. James knew many animal and bird sounds but he had no idea if Lok had experience with the same animals where he had come from. He suggested a few different bird calls and then a coyote howl. Lok's eyebrows danced with confusion along his face. Then his disposition brightened.

"Lok make noise."

The Chinaman worked up a wad of phlegm from his gut to his lungs, through his throat and rattling around in his nose. Satisfied he had gathered the proper amount of sputum, Lok released a wad of nasty fluids from deep inside his soul. The noise was certainly unique and it garnered more volume than James had expected out of simple bird whistles.

"That's disgusting but it will do."

James grinned at Lok and shooed him away with his chin nod toward the mine shaft. Lok darted about and pranced from tree to rock to clump of men until he safely reached the mine without detection of anyone pertinent to James' predicament.

As soon as Lok disappeared into the opening, James cursed himself. He realized he would never hear Lok's signal if the man were inside the mine. The deep tunnels swallowed up sound as easily as it did light. James would never get the advanced warning he needed to make it out alive. He would need to make a dash for it immediately and hope that Remus cut his losses on James' punishment for the benefit of his profits. Without being chased, James would find Carson and save him from the monster that had come to life the night before.

James grumbled again. Now that the plan had moved up in timing, James would have to go after Carson without his pistol, knife, or any help from burly men with tracking skills and copious amounts of muscle.

He was alone and would have to continue as such. James thought of Carson and he knew he had to be brave for his little buddy. Carson, too, was alone somewhere out there with a monster for a chaperone. And he was most likely scared out of his wits.

IF he was still alive, James reasoned. He shoved the notion aside and rolled to his knees before crawling under the large ferns into the forest.

Chapter Seventeen

The instant Carson opened his eyes, he thought he had been placed in an Eagle's nest. The makeshift perch sat hundreds of feet in the air, near the peak of a redwood. A puffy cirrus cloud almost tickled Carson's hair as it swam by. He risked a climb to the top of the nest, glancing down over the edge. The greenery below reminded him of a grassy carpet like he and James had cultivated around their tree fort back in Iowa.

As he crawled along the rough surface of the nest, Carson noticed how sturdy the wooden boughs had been woven together. His fears of falling to his death evaporated as he applied more pressure to the surface under his boots. The foothold felt as sturdy as solid ground. Opposite his side of the nest, the monster rested in the sunlight. The massive creature's chest rose and fell with a steady beat. Carson could tell the monster slept as soundly as he had at one time, nestled in his bed back in Iowa before he and James had undertaken their adventures.

He felt as if something watched him. Carson spun around and found two sets of eyes, barely visible above the rim of the nest. While both cone-shaped heads were several times bigger than his own, Carson knew they were not as large as the one who had spoken to him and taken him away. His heart skipped a beat momentarily, wondering if the newcomers would tear him from the nest, drag him down the tree to the ground below where they would feast on his bones. The smaller and slightly brownish monster lifted its brow in a playful manner and forced Carson to grin.

The larger, darker one slid over the edge of the nest and crawled closer to Carson. He got a quick whiff of the same stink that the large one had. It sniffed at Carson's hair and neck, raising goose flesh from the hot breath.

A shallow whoop behind him brought all the action to a halt.

MY FAMILY WISHES TO MEET YOU.

Carson focused on the smaller one as he sensed it was a child like he was. Of course, the smaller monster was as large as George in terms of height. But this creature was three times as wide across the chest and shoulders. And it was still dwarfed by the others. The monster introduced its son and wife to Carson but both names were made of such sounds that Carson could not understand what they meant in his own language. He waved at them, which confused the beasts by their returned expressions.

The monster explained how they had been chased from far lands to the east. Each time they found virgin land to settle down, the creatures were hunted by red and white man. Forced to live deep in the corners of the wild, the family had also learned to hunt and travel by night and rest by day. It spoke of related clans that lived close by. Warriors would stand guard during the sunlight so the families could rest. And when night fell, the warriors would slumber while the families hunted and secured various hiding spots for future use. They had migrated west and then north and south as needed to scrounge for more resources or lose the trail of the men who tried to harm them.

Carson felt sad when it told him tales of how they wished to be left alone and live freely like the deer and the rabbits. But their size made it difficult to remain out of sight. Their stature also engendered tremendous fear in man. Most men ran in the opposite direction when their paths crossed. However, plenty of men pursued them to the ends of the earth in a ploy to rid their loved ones of fear and danger. It named the ones who had been killed over time and the list of individuals grew so long that Carson thought he was sitting in the pew at Sunday services and listening to the preacher call out all the names of saints and descendants of Adam and Eve.

Tears streaked the smaller one's face and the mother whimpered when the monster said the final few names. A sign that it must have spoken about relatives very close to the family. Carson's chest fluttered and he trembled with sorrow as his own eyes leaked for the hairy beasts.

CAN YOU HELP US? MAN NEEDS TO KNOW WE JUST WANT TO BE LEFT ALONE.

Carson shook his head. He didn't know how he could tell the world to stop chasing these creatures. He felt horrible for calling them monsters and treating them in kind. As scary as they looked, Carson knew the hairy creatures were not unlike he and James, and Sarah and George. He wanted to invite them to come live with him but he remembered they had no home in this region. And getting the massive beings all the way back to Texas would be an impossible feat, considering how long it had taken them to travel to their current location from the farm.

"I want to help but I don't know how." Carson reached to the smaller one, tentatively at first, and then he stroked the fine hair along the lower arm. The smallish one made a horrific expression which Carson understood to be a delighted smile. It stroked Carson's hand in a caring response.

YOU WILL KNOW WHAT TO DO WHEN THE TIME COMES.

Carson nodded but he had no idea what that meant. He enjoyed the moment with the family of large beings. But he missed James and started to worry that James would never find him. He wanted to ask them if he could go back to the camp but he wasn't sure how they would react.

GOING BACK WOULD BE DANGEROUS FOR YOU. AND US.

Carson frowned. He stomped his boot heel into the wooden boughs supporting them high in the clouds. The mother being snatched him up and cradled him against her breast. She smelled like the big one but slightly less pungent. As if a garden of wildflowers had brushed against her hair.

He nestled closer to her and felt safe for the first time in days.

Carson closed his eyes and remembered his mother, how she had held him and cuddled with him in bed every night.

A tear ran down his face.

Chapter Eighteen

Massive impressions sank into the earth along what could be considered a game trail. The major difference being this trail had been forged by something that defied the laws of existence. James knelt to inspect the footprints left behind. Each marker had been pressed into the ground, causing an enormous shape reminiscent of a human foot. He estimated the prints to be seventeen inches long and approximately eight inches wide.

As James traced the print with his fingertips, his eyes wandered up the trail. Unlike most game trails, this one appeared narrower at the bottom and then widened above. He knew the reason. James had seen the monster and he shivered while his mind recalled the size of the creature.

It had been as large as the redwood trees.

James snorted at his own exaggeration. But the beast had been as big as a regular forest tree. The redwoods being what they were, served to diminish the reality of what he now understood to be true. Skunk had been right. And so had Carson. The "rumors" of the wild man to scare travelers away had been a tale with meat on its bones.

He pressed on, hoping to catch up to Carson. James swallowed down his fears for Carson's safety. But a few hours on the hunt and he had gotten no closer to finding his little friend. James wished he had thought of grabbing some water before his trek into the forest. Unfortunately, he had little time to escape the makeshift prison he had been left in before Remus discovered he had been gone.

A large limb cracked somewhere ahead.

James skidded in his tracks. He bent lower and scanned the trees. A dense, shady network of trunks and foliage carpeted the landscape. Because of the nature of the forest, looks could be deceiving. Only his own legs could sense the rise in the elevation. To the naked eye, the woods looked flat, adorned in the same greens and browns like an endless canvas painted by an exceptional artist.

He held his breath and listened for movements. James detected nothing. Not even the regular sounds of the wild. Squirrels scurrying for nuts, deer chewing browse, bob white's whistling. Nothing. Even the insects had halted their buzzing and swirling.

James noticed the air had also stood still like a steeple on a church.

Several more minutes of waiting with no signs of life, James began to move forward. He took his time, carefully stepping between roots and stone to hush his patter. James paused now and again to make sure he stayed on top of the footprints as several trails crisscrossed along the undergrowth. At one intersection, James stared up the right-hand trail. He knew how nature was random and nothing developed a pattern unless touched by man. Yet, his eyes blinked at the shape which marked the trail to the right.

Two trees had been pushed over from either side of the trail. They formed an "X" with several smaller trees or limbs stretched across the top. It looked like a gate, welcoming one towards its opening. Or warding one off like a locked barn door. James whistled to himself. An untrained observer would never notice the marker as it formed a good twenty feet above the ground. Animals would certainly not notice it as they kept their heads pointed down for food and danger. But James had hunted and he knew as a hunter, you had to take in all angles for your field of attack.

CHAPTER 18

And the wild man was clearly a predator. James nodded, reflecting on the intelligence of such a creature. His skin bristled. James understood this monster to be far more dangerous than anything he had encountered in the past. The creature thought like a man.

James deliberated over his next moves. Should he broach the threshold of the gate? Or should he avoid it at all costs? His eyes darted along the trail. It scoured the soil for the prints and what he found was the story he needed to continue his search.

The prints faded dead ahead. Whatever the gate had meant, it would hold no clues for Carson's whereabouts because the monster had maintained a straight course. James hurried along, checking prints in between quick glances to the sides of the trail for any other signs of the wild man. The silence that had enveloped him moments ago had been erased as the residents of the woods came back to life. James heard crickets and chirps. A faint whiff of air even brushed along the stubble on his cheeks.

Several hundred yards up the slow rise, the trail went cold. James dropped to his knees and carefully felt around for more footprints. The dirt remained as loose as it had back aways. So notions of compaction erasing the prints dropped away. Puzzled, James turned in tight circles on his knees. His fingers felt along the grasses and weeds along the trail, hoping to find a divot or unsettled stone to get him back on track.

But he found nothing.

He punched the ground and grumbled to himself.

"No, no, no."

Panic escalated in his gut. James knew that he was running out of time. The rescue mission had already been delayed due to his imprisonment by Skunk. And with the trail gone cold, James felt as if the clock had stopped, dead.

Not dead, James shoved the word out of his mind, afraid it would represent the status of his missing best friend.

James pulled himself up, brushing the sand from his palms along his legs. He had promised to care for Carson. And time after time, James proved his unworthiness for living up to expectations. His own as much as his mother's.

A crackle of wood high above shook James from his reflection. He shielded his eyes with the edge of his hand even though little sunshine broke through the dense canopy overhead. Nothing stirred and the foliage camouflaged whatever had made the sound. He reasoned it had been a squirrel jumping from one branch to another. But his gut told him there was more to the sound than the facts revealed.

James decided to double back and ensure that he had followed the correct set of prints. Perhaps he had missed a spot where a different set had moved in another direction. And he had ended up following the false set of prints. He rushed back to the last place he had felt confident in his tracking so he could start again.

Chapter Nineteen

Remus Phillips ground his teeth together hard enough to chip a fragment off one of his incisors. He felt his blood rise to a frothy boil as he stared down at the loosened rope where James Johnson had been bound.

"Skunk!"

The switch strained inside his fist as his grip tightened. Remus glared across the barren encampment, impatiently awaiting his foreman.

"Skunk!"

Dusty hustled down the slope from the mine shaft. He moved extremely fast for a man of his size and age. Remus stomped his heel into the ground, angered that the wrong man was approaching.

"Where is Skunk? I need Skunk." Remus waved his switch in Dusty's face as the man slid to a halt in the soft dirt.

"He's in the mine. Doing what you asked." Dusty wrenched his jaw nervously. His eyes darted from Remus to the switch. "Sir." Remus bristled at the afterthought of acknowledging his status.

"Well, go get him. Now!" Remus screamed hard enough to force a cough out of the back of his throat. Dusty nodded and turned heel to do his bidding. Halfway up the slope, Remus shouted to Dusty. "And bring me that Chink, too."

Skunk came running from the mine shaft shortly after Dusty has disappeared. He wasted little time responding to Remus' call. Skunk inspected the missing prisoner with a sour expression. It made Remus feel minutely better to see Skunk's concern.

"Where is James? I thought you tied him up."

Skunk scratched at his wild hair, nodding. "Yes, sir. I did."

Remus jammed the switch into Skunk's throat, lifting the man's chin skyward.

"Then perhaps you can explain what happened to him. Do you need a refresher in knot-tying?"

Skunk crouched down and inspected the rope. His thick fingers twisted the frayed ends in his palm.

"The rope's been cut. He was tied tighter than a virgin in church, sir."

Remus could no longer contain his hostility. He swung the switch back and forth, careful not to punish his foreman, but close enough to instill his displeasure and release pent up anger. Skunk didn't flinch once. Remus wondered if the man had little fear or if he chose to be a man among man and accept whatever punishment came has way.

"I want James found and brought to me. Alive. So I can serve him the justice he deserves."

Spittle flew from his lips. Remus dabbed the slobber away with the back of his shirt sleeve.

Dusty arrived with Lok Lee. The man's bear-sized paw wrapped firmly around the Chinaman's bicep.

"Here's the Chink, sir." Dusty shoved Lok ahead, content to stay back a few feet, outside the swing radius of the boss' weapon. Lok faltered and fell to his knees. He began to help himself up until Remus charged him with the switch held aloft.

"Remain on your knees, you cur." Remus slapped Lok across the side of the head with his whip. The stroke was hard enough to draw blood from the man's ear.

"Where is James?"

CHAPTER 19

Lok's lower lip trembled. His hat jiggled along his scalp as the fear shook his whole being.

"Lok work. Lok no see James."

Remus whipped Lok. The Chinaman flopped to the ground, clutching at his arm.

"You willing to die for that boy, Chink? Tell me where he is."

Lok gasped, cradling his arm away from another strike.

"Sir, maybe it would be best to whip his back so he can still work." Dusty kneaded his fists along his thighs. Skunk shot Dusty a cautious look.

"This filthy animal is better dead to me than living if he can't be trusted." Remus slashed down, the switch opening a bloody path across the man's face. Lok screamed, pressing his wound into his hands.

"Lok work. Lok work. No whip."

Remus stepped forward, digging his boot tip into the back of Lok's neck. He pressed down until the man gagged on dirt for air. Remus lowered himself, leaning his weight upon the boot in Lok's neck. He whispered so only Lok could hear him.

"If you help me find James then I will give you your freedom back. You'd like that, wouldn't you?"

Remus felt Lok attempt to nod beneath his boot. Satisfied he was getting what he needed, Remus released his foot from Lok. He tugged the man up to his knees so he could look him in the eyes. Lok choked and cried. Grains of sand littered his face and stuck to his tongue and eyelashes where wetness clung. Remus pressed his lips against Lok's bloody ear and whispered.

"Just tell me the truth and I will set you free. Did you help James escape?"

Lok blubbered through his native language. Remus gripped the stick in his hand, impatient for his answer.

"Did you help him? Where is he now?" Remus licked blood away from Lok's ear.

The Chinaman sunk; shoulders slumped downward. He nodded as a snot bubble popped from his nostril. "Lok no knows where James. Find brother." The response trickled out in between sobs, barely audible.

But Remus heard what he needed.

He rose to his feet and glared at Skunk and Dusty. Remus felt torn between his duty towards the family profits and his insatiable desire for vengeance. Always a slave to his emotions, Remus caved to his baser needs and hoped the business would manage itself.

"Dusty, I need you to do what it takes to keep this operation going. Deprive the men of sleep and sustenance if you must. I expect the work to be on schedule by the time I get back." He swatted the stick into his fist, signaling the ramifications if Dusty came up short.

"Skunk, you round up our best rifleman and help me track down James."

"But sir. What about the mining? Why waste time chasing him when we have so much work to do?"

Remus glared over Skunk's shoulder as Dusty ran back to the mine.

"Don't question my authority, Skunk. I'll do what I think is best for the company. And serving justice is one of my duties."

Skunk nodded hesitantly. "What about Lok?" He pointed at the bleeding, blubbering mess at their feet.

Remus chuckled. "He's coming with us. Every good hunt requires the proper bait."

Chapter Twenty

Carson giggled and splashed the youngster. He had grown comfortable with the family of wild men. They had fed Carson and carried him everywhere they went, which he thoroughly enjoyed because he got the opportunity to see the world from a new perspective. A view from the top!

Mobay, at least that's how the creature's name seemed to be pronounced, dunked himself under the surface of the river. Carson waited for his new friend to pop up so he could splash him again. The chilly water felt refreshing as it swirled around his naked frame, covering his flesh in pickled bumps. Just as Carson began to worry his friend had been under the water too long, the large hairy creature broke the surface with a plume of spray. Carson laughed hard when he noticed the trout clenched in Mobay's teeth.

"You're funnied." Carson doggy-paddled over to Mobay, wishing to take a closer look at the fish. As he neared the grinning hairy man, Mobay swung his long, muscular arms in a hugging motion, forcing a tidal wave into Carson's opened mouth and excited expression. Carson swallowed a mouthful of river water and choked, stopping abruptly in place to regain his breathing.

From the shoreline, Mobay's father chastised him for nearly drowning Carson. He apologized in Carson's mind, explaining how Mobay is used to rough housing with others his own size, not a smaller human.

They played for another hour or so before they got called back to the shore. Carson reddened and hurried for his pants, just as he had when he had stripped before swimming. The difference being the family had already been in the water when Carson had removed his clothing. So no eyes upon his nakedness. Coming out of the river, the three wild men were already sitting in the grass along the river, watching him. And his wet legs made it extremely more difficult to pull his pants up quickly. As Carson flailed and spun in circles, the family giggled with thunderous, reverberating noises which tickled Carson's chest.

Cooniketaton, the mother, had divvied up the trout into equal portions for the foursome to eat. She had tucked the meat into a leafy shell and sprinkled it with small seeds that smelled like flowers. Carson's stomach growled but he stared at the raw fish with horror. He had never eaten anything raw and the thought of chewing on the smelly fish without being cooked made him squirm. The wild men awaited Carson to take the first bite, like he had been the guest at their make-shift table. Carson hesitated and then fingered his fish sandwich. His skin turned pale when he unwrapped the leafy and found the fish's eyeball staring up at him. He gasped aloud.

IS SOMETHING WRONG?

Carson shrugged. "I never eated eyes before."

More laughter from the trio.

THE EYES ARE SPECIAL BECAUSE THEY CONTAIN THE SOUL. EATING THEM PROTECTS YOU FROM THE WATERS.

Carson wrinkled his nose. He slid his fish across the ground, trading his morsel with the wild man.

An enormous hand with rough black skin patted Carson's bare shoulder.

YOU DON'T HAVE TO EAT IT IF YOU ARE NOT COMFORTABLE.

CHAPTER 20

The wild man lifted Carson's morsel, showed it to him and then popped the whole thing into his wide mouth. He tilted his head back, enjoying the snack. When his head leaned, Carson watched as the entire torso tilted with the head, as if it was one long body part. He scratched his head and lolled his own neck in a circle to prove to himself that he had more flexibility than the wild man.

The family ate their sandwiches and sat impatiently, staring at Carson so he would eat his share. Carson felt the pressure and decided to hold his nose and swallow the meat whole. That way he would not gag on the raw flesh. When Carson dropped the fish onto his tongue, his taste buds danced with the bounty of flavor he had never tasted before. The trout tasted much milder than it smelled. And the leaf had a crunchy, bready texture with a slight nut flavor. The tiny flower seeds added a fruity afterbite which brought the whole delicacy to a refined finish. Carson's eyes bulged with happiness as he chewed the snack. He wished they had caught more trout as the snack only increased his hunger pangs.

YOU SHOULD TRUST US. I TOLD YOU IT WOULD BE GOOD.

Carson clapped his hands together and swallowed the last bit of chewed food. "I gotta showed James how to make that. It was yummied."

They rested in the sunshine, drying their thick coats of long hair. Carson felt dry as well but his crotch was still wet and the dungarees chafed his inner thighs when he walked. He silently complained to himself that he should have dried off before pulling on his pants. The wild man had listened in on his mind and plucked Carson from the ground. He perched the boy on his shoulder and stomped forward without skipping a beat. Carson felt his stomach rise to his throat and drop back down like he had jumped off a quarry ledge. Once his belly settled, he clutched his fist into the wild man's long hair and held on as the trees whipped past them. The wild men walked like horses ran, the world rushing by with little effort.

Carson smiled and shouted with glee, trying to slap branches high above the ground below. While the parents walked, Mobay climbed redwood tree trunks and swung from branch to branch. Sometimes he would jump from trunk to trunk like a gigantic squirrel, unafraid of falling and sure of grip. Carson wished he could do the same thing. He imagined how much fun he would have if he could move as fast, escaping notice and hiding from James. Carson's world opened wide to the possibilities he could only dream of prior to meeting the wild men.

WE STILL HAVE SO MUCH TO SHOW YOU.

Carson nodded subconsciously to the voice which talked inside his head. It had become second nature to communicate with the creatures through his thoughts. What had scared him in the beginning had turned into a means of convenience. Carson clenched his eyes shut and spoke inside his head.

FASTER? OKAY, WE WILL GO FASTER.

Carson felt the monstrous shoulders hefting his weight chug forward with an extra burst of speed. He opened his eyes and watched the scenery go by in a blur.

"Yeah!" Carson held both hands in the air, enjoying the rise and fall of his excitement deep within his belly.

Chapter Twenty-one

All signs led James to the same conclusion. He was lost and had gotten no closer to finding Carson. The forest terrain resembled a house of mirrors. Each tree looked the same as another. The undergrowth hid lesser travel byways and the well-worn game trails provided little clues beyond the large footprints he had found.

James fanned his sweaty face with his hat. Deep within the bowels of the forest, the air had become cloying and thick. Whatever minor breeze James had encountered early in his search had evaporated like a rain puddle in the noon-day sun. James hoped to find his friend before nightfall. Time was running out and his gut wrenched at the thought of Carson missing for so long. And with the nightfall coming, his chances of finding a way out of the redwoods would dwindle.

A rock thumped the ground near his feet. James danced a two-step, an automatic reaction to the surprise. He ducked against a tree and scoured the surroundings. James knew of no creature that could grip and throw a rock besides another human being. Or a wild man. Closing his eyes, James focused his attention on the sounds around him. The woods had been silent. Not even a bird or insect moved.

The shrill scream startled James. He jumped up and ran as the noise frightened him away from his spot of safety. James cupped his ears as he ran, imagining a woman being slaughtered at the hands of a madman. Another stone whizzed past his face as he darted amongst the redwoods. James hunkered down into a new position. The scream, so loud and piercing and so long-winded it would require massive lungs, tailed off. James regrouped his courage and he stood to face the thing that haunted him.

"Come out and fight me like a man." James shouted with all his might. His fingers tapped against his hip, an old habit of feeling for his pistol. He cursed himself for challenging the beast when he was powerless to defend himself. No pistol. No knife.

Several whoops echoed from around James. One response from his left, another from his right. The third response came from behind him. James spun, expecting to see a towering monster before him. Instead, a treetop full of leaves and as thick as his own waist began swaying gently as if a hurricane wind had gusted into the canopy. Within moments, the tree shook violently. The motion was impossible under ordinary circumstances. Even more so as no other tree in the forest moved at all.

James hightailed it in the direction from which no whoops had come. He stumbled over hidden roots and ignored the scratches of branches that jutted in his way like bony fingers of the dead come to snatch him up. The forest around him thundered and crashed. The ground beneath his boots quaked and rumbled like the earth shifted into a sinkhole. Branches snapped in violent explosions, gaining on him from all angles. James wished he had taken more time to collect his gun before he had run off to find Carson. Images of Carson, alone and crying, flooded James' mind. He had managed to lose his best friend and get himself killed as well. James quickly blinked away thoughts of Carson, only to be overwhelmed with scenes of his mother receiving the news that he and Carson had died. Sarah broke down, dropping to her knees, the teardrops soaking the letter which informed her of her losses.

The forest broke open and James found a river rushing downhill. The bank fell away before his legs caught up with his brain. James toppled a dozen feet off the ledge into the ice-cold water. As fast as he sunk beneath the tide, James resurfaced to find himself drifting downstream. He snatched his soaked hat from getting away while more rocks rained down upon him from above. James glared over his right shoulder for signs of the beasts but the trees blotted out any shapes of beings. The stones ceased plunking into the water around him. James allowed the current to take him a bit further before he would swim for the other shoreline. After being stifled inside the redwoods, the icy water felt refreshing.

James swam for the far bank, struggling against the flow. He grabbed for some deadfalls but his fingers failed to gain a hold. The current slowed at a wider expanse where James felt the bottom rise. His boots touched the large rocks below and James slogged his way toward the shore. Exhausted and soaked through, James flopped onto the sandy surface before clawing his way onto the grass. Arms outstretched, James blinked at the sky, enjoying the warm rays piercing his soggy clothes. He took off his boot and turned it upside down. A gush of water splashed upon the ground. James removed the other boot and tossed it a few yards away, too tired to pour its contents out.

Once he caught his breath, James took inventory of the area. Dense foliage across the river from where had come. Matching forest on his side of the river. He glanced up and down the waterway, amazed at how it had cut a clear path through the endless forest. With a source of direction now in hand, James felt more confident he could find his way out of the woods. The river would end up somewhere - at some point. He would keep the river within earshot as best he could to maintain his bearings. And James knew animals required water to survive. If the wild men had Carson, then they would be close to a source of water like this river. His goal would be to find where the wild men dwelled. If he could locate the wild men, then James would find Carson.

"Hang on, buddy. I'm coming for you." James spoke to nobody but himself.

As he gathered his boots, James got a whiff of something stinky. He pinched his nose, attempting to identify the culprit. When he stood in his squishy boots, James noted several depressions in the soil. The grass had been matted down in three semi-circles. One large indentation followed by a smaller one. Across from those two was an enormous section of crushed ground. James bent down and sniffed the patterns. His head shot back in disgust. He recognized the odor from the monster that had broken through the encampment.

"Carson."

James rubbed his hand outside the largest spot, feeling for a smaller clue that would confirm Carson had been here recently. He looked too the redwoods and fanned out in search of fresh footprints.

Chapter Twenty-two

Remus Phillips forced Lok to take point. After all, he was the one who knew where James went. Following closely behind Lok was McCourty, the ace sharpshooter in the outfit. The man had been known to drop officers from one hundred yards at Gettysburg. Skunk had vouched for McCourty's skills with a Winchester, enumerating the large game he had bagged along the journey from the east coast.

Skunk trod alongside Remus. The hunt for James Johnson had been absent of conversation. Remus preferred to mind his business, not in the sense of keeping to himself. However, more in the vein of contemplating his future moves. His mind toiled with increasing the company's profitability, thus enamoring himself in the eyes of his daddy while simultaneously outshining his incorrigible brother, Romulus. Twins at birth, the boys had been anything but similar. Remus was strong and calculating. Romulus was delicate and reactive. About the only similarity besides their bloodline was their hair-trigger tempers. Romulus would stomp and argue when set upon. Remus would put out a man's eye just for looking at him improperly.

Remus whistled. The posse halted as Remus pushed his way toward the front. Lok cowered which heightened the boss' enjoyment. He slapped the switch against his leg to solicit an extra flinch out of the Chinaman.

"Where is he? We've come a long way and you have yet to prove we are on the right track."

Lok shrugged. "Lok look. No boots. This trail." His outstretched hand indicated curving game trail they had been hiking since they discovered it.

Remus lashed across Lok's chest. The small man dropped to the ground, clutching at his new wound.

"I swear you Chinks ain't worth a spit." He raised the switch once more, poised to strike again.

"These woods are vast. James could be anywhere. McCourty, you see any signs along the way?" Skunk stood between Remus and Lok.

"Couple boot prints, here and there. Not much to go on though."

Remus clenched his jaw, speaking through his teeth. "Not much to go on? How many boots you think come stomping through these parts on a regular basis? Hm? This is the last place that men have ventured to and I damn well expect if there's prints then they belong to that rascal."

It irked him to stare into the blank face of the sharpshooter. Remus had hoped McCourty would sass him so he could levy more violence from the end of his whip. All he got in return was a dumb, Kentucky hillbilly expression.

"I'll take point with McCourty so we can speed up the search." Skunk patted the sharpshooter's arm.

"Do you take me for an imbecile? Leaving me back here with the Chink so he can run off? I'd just as soon kill him and leave him for the coyotes." Remus shoved Skunk out of his way and hovered over Lok. The small man used his hands to cover his head from the upcoming blows. "I decide what we do and you will do what I say."

The fire burned through his veins. Remus felt the urge to release his vitriol upon the posse. But he chose to start with Lok. Remus swung the switch downward in rapid succession. Each blow landing with a wet slapping sound. Rivulets of blood oozed through the fabric of the Chinaman's shirt. Lok wailed. He rolled along the ground, failing to avoid the next strike.

"Hey!"

CHAPTER 22

Remus ignored the shout. He swung and missed when Lok crawled to escape. Remus started kicking Lok in the ribs, the rage totally consuming him to the point where he would use any means possible to punish the man.

"Hey!"

Skunk grabbed Remus' wrist with vulture-like talons. He held a finger before his lips as if to quiet Remus.

"Unhand me you stinking animal." Remus wriggled to get free but could not shake the bigger man's grip. He spun outward and tried to free his switch from one hand to the other.

Remus followed their eyes as Skunk and McCourty squinted toward the right of the trail. McCourty sighted down his rifle as he scanned the forest.

"What is it?" Breathing heavily, Remus yanked his arm free of Skunk. The three men stared in the same direction. Lok whimpered behind them, a ball of blood and sweat.

"I think that was James." Skunk whispered.

"James? What was James?"

"The 'hey' we just heard. It came from over there." Skunk used his finger to draw Remus' attention to a more specific direction. Remus heard his own heartbeat pounding inside his ears. The excitement of killing James and returning to the mine as quickly as they could would be a major relief. He vaguely recalled someone shouting as he bludgeoned Lok, but he had assumed it had been Skunk attempting to save the hapless soul.

"If you want to beat on someone, maybe you should be on me."

An icy chill ran up his spine. The voice belonged to James. But he couldn't see him. The forest was so thick and the tops of the trees had begun to cast dark shadows as the day transformed toward dusk.

Remus stepped forward.

"Come out, James. I just wish to talk about our disagreement. I promise you will not be tied up again."

Silence.

Skunk cleared his throat as if here were about to speak but Remus shushed him.

"If you show yourself then I will consider it an act of good faith and we will help you look for Carson."

More silence.

McCourty moved the rifle barrel back and forth in search of any movement. Skunk turned sideways like he needed to point his ears nearer the forest. Remus rapped his switch quietly against his leg to satisfy his urge to explode with anger. The tapping sound kept steady beat with his breathing.

"If you don't come forward then I will be forced to kill Lok. And his blood will be on YOUR hands. You're the reason he is being punished, James."

Remus waited impatiently. His eyes clicked in the sockets, darting across the landscape for his quarry. The switch handle creaked beneath his tightening grip.

"Damn you, James. I will kill you and your simpleton brother. But first, I will show you my wrath, show you the consequences of your behavior."

Remus returned to Lok. He threw up his arm, poised in the air with the whip dangling behind him, taunting one last time to draw James from his hiding spot. After a moment which felt like an eternity, Remus did what he loved to do most in life.

Chapter Twenty-three

The fire in his belly torched him from the inside out. James clenched his fists as he peeked through the foliage at Remus. With his switch held high, Remus glowered in James' general direction, clearly attempting to stir the pot so James would give up his location. But James was prepared to wait the boss out.

Remus brought his weapon down repeatedly, slashing his fury through Lok's flesh. With his attention diverted, James mobilized his attack. He sprung from the dense underbrush and sprinted into the fray. His stealth and speed caught Skunk by surprise, especially as the enormous man had been drawn to Lok's penance. James leaped forward like a bison charging a tribe of hunters, his head tucked low and right shoulder braced for contact.

Remus never saw him coming.

The switch flew from his clenched fist as it swung back for another swipe. James and Remus collapsed in a spray of soil and greenery. Their bodies intermingled with sweat and hostility. As James rolled off Remus, he crouched to his haunches like a mountain line primed to get his prey. Remus clenched his jaw and rose to deliver his response to the surprise fight. James anticipated Remus' kick, almost seeing the leg swing back before it did. He grasped the upturned boot and spun it with all his might. Remus flipped over to his left.

"James." Skunk swung his hand upwards, knocking McCourty's rifle away. The sharpshooter had aimed his gun at James with his finger on the trigger.

Remus scrabbled to his feet. His nostrils flared like a steer on the Chisholm. He bent forward over his knees to prepare for another round.

"Stay out of this. James is mine."

Skunk and McCourty stepped outside the danger zone but remained close enough to intervene should Remus lose the battle.

James took advantage of Remus' lack of focus. He stepped into his punch, throwing a left jab which connected with Remus' chin. The man's furry red eyebrows slid up his forehead with amazement at being struck. As he faltered backwards, James rushed in to finish the man off. He swung his right fist far behind his ear and threw all his weight behind it.

He missed by a yard and his momentum carried him all the way down to the ground.

Remus recovered quickly. After a cursory glance for his lost switch, Remus drove a knee into James' kidney. The shot crippled James. He flailed with his right arm behind his back, doing little to provide his internal organs with comfort. Remus straddle James, using his forearms to force James' face into the earth.

He struggled to get air as Remus shouted obscenities into the back of his head. James tried to throw his head backwards but the man's strength allowed no such movement. James flailed. He heard the men behind him, McCourty encouraging Remus to finish him off. Skunk took no side but shouted his support to nobody. James envisioned Carson once more. The boy's sad face, lost and all alone in the vast wilderness of northern California. Without James to care for him, Carson would be abused by ruffians and perverts. That's if he had survived being kidnapped by the wild man. The will to overcome all odds for the sake of Carson's safety swelled in James' chest. He bucked and tossed Remus over his head, using the man's forward-leaning weight against him.

CHAPTER 23

James decided to escape before he lost his chances to do so. His temper had gotten the best of him and he knew fighting three armed men was not a good decision. As much as he wished to make Remus pay for his sins, James wanted to live to fight another day.

And to find Carson before it was too late.

He charged up the game trail and ducked beneath some thick brambles, disappearing from sight. Behind, James heard Remus command the men to pursue him. Skunk protested the waste of time with nightfall coming.

James stopped short, dropping under a deadfall, and listening for Lok. He realized one of the reasons he jumped Remus had been to save Lok. Instead, James had only saved himself. His gut wrenched with images of his poor friend taking more beatings. Lok had been dragged into the sordid mess by James. And now he had abandoned the man.

Remus and Skunk argued their options while McCourty used his barrel to pick through the woods in search of James. Rather than await his discovery, James steeled himself to make the choice to run far and look for Carson. He prayed for Lok as he ran, hoping the Chinaman could survive to work another day in the mines. James promised himself he would return, with Carson at his side, to free Lok from the shackles of his employment. Money or not, James would do what he could get Lok back to his family and miles from the dark soul of Remus Phillips.

The Winchester boomed, shocking James from his thoughts. He huffed as he climbed over boulders and ducked under branches to put more distance between himself and the hunting party. The errant shot had either been a misfire or McCourty had mistaken a creature of the forest for James because the bullet avoided his direction altogether.

As he ran, James found himself back in the same position. Alone in the forest with no weapons. And not a clue as to Carson's whereabouts. He pushed himself forward since he had covered as much of the ground behind him as he could. Carson had to be somewhere ahead. But how far? And at what point would James give up and turn back? Finding Carson in the redwoods would be like separating a different grain of sand from the rest. Everything looked the same. An endless sea of green and brown. With danger all around - bears and snakes, wolves and coyotes. Plus, an evil maniac nipping at his heels, hell bent on bringing James to his unlawful sense of justice.

James centered his internal compass on the sounds of the river to his right and the steady rise in elevation as he pointed north. He groaned as he noticed the shift in light, angling through the canopy. In less than an hour or two, James would be surrounded by a pitch-black forest.

And wild men, too.

Chapter Twenty-four

The time spent with the wild man's family had been lots of fun. Carson had learned more about the world in the last day than he had in thirteen years. He had overcome some of his shyness and discovered new flavors to delight his palate. On top of it all, Carson had made a new friend in Mobay. The "boys" had been left to their own to climb and swim and investigate the woods. A complete adventure without chores and labor. And free of James' newer adult sensibilities.

Carson had noticed the change in James since they had departed Dodge City. James had gotten serious. He preferred to spend more energy on grown-up activities instead of playing with Carson. Gone were the days of hiding from adults, playing war and cards. Even their conversations had changed. James quickly changed subjects and blathered on about his goals. At one time, James had discussed THEIR plans for travel and adventure.

It felt like Carson had become a son rather than a friend.

He sobbed and flicked a tear away. Carson faced away from them so his sorrow would go unnoticed.

WHAT SADDENS YOU?

Carson stiffened. He snorted up his runny nose and rubbed the water from his eyes with the palms of his fists. Carson tried to close his mind from thoughts so the wild man would stay out of his business.

It was futile.

YOU MISS YOUR BROTHER.

Carson gave in, nodding. He tossed a twig from the nest over the side. Carson silently counted to ten before it struck the ground below.

WE CAN RETURN YOU. JUST TELL US WHEN YOU WOULD LIKE TO LEAVE.

He remembered chasing Mobay across a flat opening in the hillside. No matter how hard he tried, he could not catch the creature. Long strides and fluid effort evaded Carson's chase each time. He smiled as he pictured Mobay spitting water in a plumed fountain over Carson's head when they swam in the river.

YOU MISS HOME YET YOU WISH TO STAY.

Carson swiveled on his butt to face the wild man. Cooniketaton and Mobay slid closer, setting behind the massive father. Their eyes drooped as they paid attention to Carson's problem. He nodded.

"I needed James. I miss him so much."

WHAT IF BOTH WORLDS EXISTED TOGETHER?

Carson sat up. He would love it for James and the wild men to live as one big family. James could protect them all and maybe Sarah and George could join them, too. Carson rubbed hands along his dungarees, excited by the possibilities. He wondered if George would handle coexisting with these creatures. Sarah and James would bite but George could be difficult to understand.

The wild man mumbled under his breath, incoherently. The sound vibrated Carson's Adam's apple. His nose and ears tickled.

SOME WHITE MEN CANNOT BE REASONED WITH.

Carson shooed his thoughts of George, knowing he had lowered his defenses again.

"James will understanded. He's like me."

Mobay spoke in the language of the wild man. His parents waved their hands as they quibbled over whatever Mobay had said. A spirited debate danced back and forth until the father grunted. His vocalization shook the nest, and for a moment, Carson's belly swung up to his neck with that tickling sensation like he had felt as they ran through the forest. The feeling was both exhilarating and frightening simultaneously.

MOBAY WISHES FOR YOU TO STAY FOREVER.

Carson grinned at Mobay. He loved his new friend. As he stared at Mobay, Carson remembered his desire to be with James again. His smile faltered.

"But James." Carson's voice drifted off.

WOMEN AND CHILDREN ARE DRIVEN BY EMOTIONS. ONLY MEN CAN BE GROUNDED.

Carson pictured a room full of grown men pouting, not being allowed outside. The wild man squinted as he tried to understand how Carson's mind had conjured such a scene.

WE WILL BRING YOU BACK. THEN YOUR BROTHER CAN DECIDE THE OUTCOME.

He stroked Carson's hair, his hand covering three-quarters of Carson's scalp.

REMEMBER TO TELL WHITE MEN WE ARE TO BE LEFT ALONE. TO LIVE FREE LIKE THEY WISH TO LIVE.

Carson shook his head. He punched his leg with a closed fist.

"Bad guys will have to be fighted. Evil everywhered."

The wild man extended his thin, black lips as if kissing the air. The lips peeled back to reveal the giant, white teeth. His head nodded, understanding the truth of Carson's words.

MUST STILL TRY. NEVER GIVE UP.

The conversation faded as Cooniketaton and Mobay gathered the plants they had collected earlier. In minutes, a fragrant salad of greens, sprinkled with ants and grubs sat on bark plates before them. Carson scrunched his nose as he watched the ants darting along the leaves. His stomach roiled at the slimy, white, and yellow grubs which curled and wiggled along the plants. He watched in horror as the family unit wasted little time slurping their meals down. Once the bark plates were empty, the trio noisily chomped and ground their meals between enormous molars. They grinned sheepishly at Carson while he fidgeted with everything nearby except his supper.

Mobay picked the grubs off Carson's plate, popping them into the air and catching them on his outstretched tongue, one by one. Without the grubs and most of the ants crawling away from his plate, Carson hurried the salad into his mouth, stuffing it into his cheeks with both hands. He dropped the bark as fast as he could, afraid one of the insects would jump up to his lips. He made a yummy noise as the flavors of the indigenous flora co-mingled with his saliva.

WE WILL LEAVE SOON.

Carson bobbed his head, ecstatic to see James soon. The delicious meal enhanced his happiness.

He swiped as his chin as it tickled him. His cheeks began to itch as well. Carson rubbed at his face to satisfy the urge. He glanced at his hand and shouted in terror. A colony of ants ran along his wrist. More tickling along his face signaled the insects that he had thought he had avoided had been in his mouth.

Carson jumped up and danced frantically to bounce the bugs off his body.

The family of wild men laughed as they watched Carson lose his mind, stomping across the nest.

Chapter Twenty-five

Skunk had argued with Remus. He concluded they should cut their losses and head back to the mine. James and Carson could be chalked up as part of their losses from the invasion of wild men. Skunk reasoned they should act with haste to collect the precious ore and get out of the redwoods as soon as possible.

"I'm the boss. And I make the decisions. James must be dealt with." Remus wiped excess saliva from his lips. "McCourty, see to it that you shoot to wound, not kill. I will finish him off."

McCourty nodded, dumbfounded expression intact. Remus wanted to slap the stupid off the man's face.

"What about Lok?" Skunk scratched at his black and white mane. He bent to help the Chinaman to his feet.

"Forget the Chink. Let the wolves have him."

Skunk began to protest once more. Remus lifted his switch and the argument ended as soon as he made overtures for a whipping. Skunk jutted his chin. Remus read it as a sign of defiance and he made a mental note to deal with Skunk once they finished their business in the forest.

There will be plenty of hell to pay at the mine, Remus thought.

They followed James' path along the game trail. Even as light faded from the confines of the forest, Remus could see the distinct boot prints. Ahead, the tracks drifted into the brush and Remus pushed McCourty forward with the handle of his whip. Skunk assumed the rear in case James circled back around and attempted another sneak attack. The footing grew difficult, the steady incline of the terrain coupled with thicker vegetation and darker shadows made travel slow to an irritating pace. Remus bit his cheek against screaming with frustration. He fought to maintain a semblance of control and he refused to reveal his progress for James.

We will surprise him like he did us, Remus grumbled.

Darkness had settled under the treetops, increasing the difficulty of their journey. Several times, Remus considered calling off the chase and sheltering for the night. But his vengeance would not rest until he had meted out his full violence. Besides, he reminded himself, James will have as much trouble with the darkness as us. Hopefully, he will bed down and we will identify his camp. The stupid kid will probably light a big fire like a beacon for all to see.

The forest came alive with a thunderous roar. Skunk threw himself upon Remus as the pair collapsed into an ocean of ferns. McCourty dropped to a knee and took aim, using his sights to locate James.

Deafening sounds of large branches snapping like sticks and ungodly shrieks filled their ears. The men clasped their heads to keep their sanity from the chaos. Each scream shook their innards like a steamship's horn blast at close range.

"Get off me, you oaf." Remus shook the large man from his back. He crept to a safe position against a redwood, peeking around the edge in the direction of the sounds. His hands shook as a war raged within the woods. Shadows streaked across the landscape, barely visible in the dark. Remus swallowed a lump of bile that threatened to reverse course. With small numbers in the pitch black, so far from camp, Remus felt like a tiny rodent in the presence of the monsters which had sacked their outfit.

"Shoot them." Remus shouted.

"No. You'll give away our position." Skunk waved off McCourty as if the man could see his signal.

CHAPTER 25

Remus quietly agreed with Skunk. His fear fed the orders but hiding could better save their hides.

"Where is Carson?"

Remus froze. His shoulders hunched forward as he strained to listen closely. The voice had sounded like James. He tried to estimate how long they had been hiking and if they could have overtaken the kid's progress.

A body sailed through the scenery, brushing the tops of the ferns, and leaving them in a cascading silent wave. The body thumped into an over-sized root that grew in a gnarled knot above the soil. Remus heard the grousing of the beaten man. He recognized the voice as that of his prey. His tongue licked at smiling lips, enjoying the sounds of James' demise. He wished he could take it all in but the accursed night had robbed him of potentially the happiest moment of his adult life.

"Where? Carson. Not gonna." James spoke in choppy spurts, his strained breathing revealing massive trauma.

"Give up."

Remus slid up the tree, hazarding a better view of the destruction. Gigantic shapes shot through the trees. He couldn't be sure if there were many creatures or if the one or two had appeared to multiply because of their speed of movement. Remus pulled Skunk's collar closer. He whispered against the large man's face.

"Go ahead and make sure he is dead."

The roars and thumping earth beneath their feet dwindled as the monsters got farther away. Remus began to feel less inhibited by fear. He shoved Skunk again.

"Go."

McCourty and Skunk disappeared into the black ink. Remus waited an eternity for their return. He began to shuffle forward when Skunk and McCourty nearly bumped into him. Remus got the confirmation he needed.

James was dead.

Remus asked them to drag the body over so he could confirm the good news. But Skunk insisted they either take turns sleeping and keeping lookout or get on the trail back to the mine. He reminded Remus about their schedule and how they were already far behind. Remus pushed past Skunk to get visual confirmation when a beefy hand crunched around his bicep and held him in place. Remus could have sworn his feet came off the ground.

"Would you rather those monsters find us here? Or live to tell the tales how we survived multiple attacks and still brought your father the treasure trove of all time?"

Remus chewed on the suggestion. In his heart he knew Skunk was thinking clearly. Doing what was best for them and the company. But in his gut, Remus had unfinished business. He would never be satisfied without taking a souvenir of flesh with him as proof that James Johnson had gone straight to Hell. His mind weighed the options.

"Fine. Let's go. I don't want to be here when those things figure out we're in their neighborhood." He ordered McCourty to lead the way. Remus told Skunk to keep an eye on their rear again.

"If anyone asks, it was I who took his life. Understand?"

Remus grinned as his partners agreed to his lies. The tall tale would do more to solidify his power over the miners. And power could be worth more than gold at times.

Chapter Twenty-six

James had hunkered down for the night as the darkness had surrounded him. The redwoods blotted out most of the sunset and left him to his other senses for survival. He figured it best to grab a few hours of sleep before continuing his expedition to find Carson. The thought of sleeping seemed remote as the forest took on creepy attributes. And he had forgotten the monsters that stole Carson from him either. Chances were good that James would encounter the creatures along the way. Especially if they still held Carson against his will.

A soft hoot came from his left. James hadn't been near many owls but the sound reminded him of how an owl might sound if it were the size of a horse.

Or larger.

In response, an abnormal bird call filled the void from his right. The hair along his arm stood as James suddenly felt like he was in the company of others. Dangerous others. He strained his eyes for movement along his field of vision. The interplay of shadows and natural motions within the forest played games with his mind. He found it difficult to discern what was moving due to night currents versus something that wished him harm.

James poked his head above the brush. A knock drew his attention. It sounded like a stick being struck along a tree trunk. The knock had been followed by a whoop on the other side. He recalled hearing such noises when the encampment had been invaded by the monsters. His blood ran cold as the realization that something was about to happen alerted him.

The earth shook under his bottom. It felt as if the ground rose and dropped each time the loud noise happened. Like a herd of wild horses ran by, except the horses weighed thousands of pounds. James' eyes darted back and forth, deceived by the disparate sounds mixed with the sense of dark shapes running rampant. The thunderous crashing circled him and drew nearer. He imagined a wagon train wrapping around and around, rolling faster with reckless abandon like the horses that drew them teetered on the brink of sanity.

James began to crawl back under the deadfall when an enormous, leathery hand snatched him off the soil and carried him like a sagging bag of seed. He tried to squirm from the grip but the strength in the hand outdid all his efforts. The stench of human body odor combined with a full outhouse in the noon-day sun of July and caressed with the decaying corpses of sunbaked deer choked the air from his lungs. James choked back vomit as he tried to focus on what was happening.

The chaos had come on so quickly. James had little time to think of helping himself let alone what he could be up against. But he knew. The calls. The smell. The total whirlwind of mayhem. James understood the monsters had found him. He just needed to get Carson away from them.

James bit into the arm that tucked him into the hairy flesh. The monster dropped him to the ground. James thudded to a stop along the brush. He realized by the impact that he had been higher off the ground than he had known. The wind had sailed from his mouth and he gasped to recover. Before he could get air, another monster lifted him with both hands and threw him forward like a schoolyard child tossing a ball. James crashed into a redwood, the back of his head colliding with the smooth, solid bark first. The night grew bright as white lightning filled his vision as his mind worked to shake the cobwebs.

CHAPTER 26

He drifted in and out of consciousness, listening to the shrieks and destruction all around. James counted at least three creatures by the cadence and distance of their steps. He struggled to determine if one of the monsters was smaller or if they were farther away because the crashing sounds of the feet differed.

Getting thrown and beaten, James attempted to speak with the creatures. His last hope had been to reason with the monsters since he could do little to battle them on equal ground. The wild men either failed to understand his language or they ignored him outright. He fought to call out to Carson. James hoped Carson was with the beasts so he could hear his voice and know his little friend was alive. All he got was grunts and huffs and strange chatter. Everything unintelligible.

James landed upside down. His teeth clacked together and he tasted blood. The world swooned and James knew he was about to succumb to his injuries. Death weaved its way into his being, collapsing his will and usurping his energy. He stared at the stars that twinkled high above, revealing just enough shine for James to recognize them as real. The black air closed in, fuzzing the edges of his vision before dunking it deep inside his brain which continued to slosh its way to a stop in his skull. Even the sounds of the monsters washed away, like a gentle gurgle of water along a rocky creek. He teared as he watched his mother toil on the farm in her old age. George was there, too. But he had withered to a hunched old man, leaning on a hickory walking stick to support his massive frame.

Carson wasn't on the farm.

James saw the boy strewn along the carpet of forest. Maggots used his head for a hotel and spiders crawled under the fabric of his clothing. A black magpie swooped down and ate unimpeded of his friend's delicate meat. Carson would have lived to a ripe age on the farm with his mother and George if James had only listened to their pleas. His ego battled reason. As beautiful as it had felt to have a home, a place they could own and work,

James had never been content with routine. Now he longed for it. But it was too late.

James counted the beats of his heart. The rhythm mimicked his breathing, slowing down and growing softer. He wondered if there would be anything left, a part of his being found so it could be placed at rest.

He wished he could be buried under the tree fort Carson and he had dug out back in Pella. How simple life had been back then.

Life.

James dreamed of life as hot tears flooded his sockets. He paid close attention to the path each drop took as it ran across his flesh.

I paid attention, Carson.

Chapter Twenty-seven

Carson sat quietly on the wild man's shoulder as they trudged through the darkness. The rhythmic trek lulled him to sleep periodically. At least, until the wild man needed to duck or shift his balance to accommodate the terrain. Then Carson would snap awake.

His mind had been flooded with conflicts between memories and life as he had known it and the new enlightenment he had achieved with the introduction of his new friends. He could never go back to a time when he had been so innocent, so unaware of the world around him. Carson had learned plenty along the trail - differences between cities and peoples. He had witnessed the miracles of life as well as the depravities that mankind could create. But the wild men brought so much more to his experiences. Mostly, they had taught him to listen more closely to nature and to understand others before judging them.

The goodbyes had been long and painful. Carson had cried as he hugged Mobay. The long, hairy arms squeezed the breath from his chest. For the first time in his life, Carson had made a friend that he could play with and feel like equals. James had been by Carson's side since he was a baby, but James was more like family. They had grown up together because of their mothers' profession. Not forced to be friends but revolving in each other's circle because of circumstances. The children in the schoolyard made fun of Carson. They teased him and pushed him around. Even the teacher treated him differently which only reinforced the attitudes of his classmates. Mobay took Carson in. He didn't take advantage of Carson or point out his inadequacies. In fact, Mobay had behaved as if Carson was a wild man himself. If Carson had struggled to keep up, Mobay would encourage him and allow him to fail. Still reassuring Carson to try harder the next time.

Harder than saying goodbye to Mobay was letting go of Cooniketaton. She had embraced Carson as a member of the family. Her hugs and gentility reminded Carson how badly he missed his own mother. Sarah had picked up where his mommy had left off and Carson loved Sarah just the same. Deep inside, he knew Sarah wasn't his mother though. And Cooniketaton went out of her way to make him feel as comfortable as if he were home. She provided Carson with a home, temporary within the redwood forest, but a home, nonetheless. Her nurturing soothed his soul when he felt blue or scared.

Carson had held his goodbyes for the wild man until he returned to the mining camp with James. He could not stomach a third, sorrowful display of neediness. Plus, he had taken too long wrapping things up with the other two. The wild man wanted to get Carson back before sunrise to avoid additional confrontations. He explained why his clan had leveled the camp. The wild men had been pushed from east to west as white men spread across the land. They had been hunted and chased like the buffalo and the rest of the creatures of the forest. With little room left to hide, they agreed to make their stand against the scourge of mankind. One of the reasons there had been so little activity in the redwoods had been their ability to scare off mountain men, miners, railroad barons. All who encountered the aggression turned tail and went back the way they had come. Every so often, the wild men met white men who refused to run. Men driven by greed and morality that ignored the land and the beasts that inhabited it.

And they hoped to do the same with the Phillips Mining Company.

Carson's appeal saved the miners from total wanton destruction. The wild man felt how special Carson was and he wanted to use Carson's purity to spread the clan's message. An offer to coexist without interference. The wild man begged Carson to understand their plight. He helped Carson rehearse the cause so it would flow easily from his lips.

The night reinforced Carson's somberness. Darkness clouded the forest and cloaked his outlook for the future of the species. Carson was smart enough to know that men could hardly be trusted. He had seen them behave like overlords of God's creatures.

THERE IS ALWAYS HOPE.

Carson stroked the back of the wild man's head. His jagged fingernails got tangled in some strands of long hair and he freed them without yanking the follicles from the scalp. He leaned his head against the mane of hair, crushing the side brim of his hat. As tears threatened to return, Carson switched his thoughts to James. He had pangs in his heart since he had always been near James as far back as he could remember. Apart, Carson enjoyed his adventure with the wild men but he needed to see James. Carson had to be close to his best friend to feel normal again.

They arrived at the bend in the river where the trail cut directly southeast towards the mining camp. The wild man lowered Carson so he could take a moment to relieve himself. Carson decided to do the same since he had no idea how much longer they still had to travel. As they finished, the wild man clutched Carson tight and lifted him to eye level.

DON'T CHANGE, CARSON. THE WORLD NEEDS MORE OF YOU.

Carson chuckled nervously. He didn't understand the comment, shrugging it off as meaning something nice. The wild man placed Carson back atop his massive shoulder. He pushed branches from their path as the trail became congested. Carson held on tight.

NOT MUCH LONGER.

Butterflies filled Carson's belly like he was about to meet a pretty girl for the first time. He worried James wouldn't be happy to see him. Carson realized he had been having fun but James had not come to find him. More fears crept into his head. Had James been relieved to get rid of Carson? Did he forget all about his little friend? Was James okay?

His hands shook and an icy sweat broke out along the back of his neck.

Carson prayed he was wrong about James.

Chapter Twenty-eight

Heavy rumbles brought their procession to a halt. The rush of danger unfurled on them with no warning. The forest exploded like a storm of the century. Trees swayed and branches snapped like thunder. They scattered in all directions as the men fled for their lives.

Remus threw himself into a thorny patch of growth. Each point tearing cloth and skin like razor wire. He bit his lower lip to stifle an outburst of pain.

Skunk shouted from across the path. Remus couldn't understand what he had said with the din all around them. The ground shook and undulated as the enormous beasts crashed through the forest.

Deafening screams came from everywhere at once. Remus twitched and buried his head in his chest. He trembled, afraid he would be discovered and tossed around like James. A gunshot echoed between the trees, the bullet ricocheting above his position.

"Watch out!" Remus admonished himself for calling attention to his hiding spot.

Skunk lunged in front of Remus. He landed on his belly, face to face with the boss.

"They're everywhere." No sooner had the words escaped Skunk's mouth and he had been dragged backwards by his feet. Remus heard the man's nails scrape along the earth for purchase as he was pulled away. Then the screams confirmed his capture by the hairy beasts.

"McCourty. Fire at will." Remus rose to his knees. Shadows darted between gaps in the forest. Remus swore he counted dozens of monsters treading through their field of view. He searched for McCourty, squinting to make out the man's slovenly shape.

The rifle boomed.

Remus sprang from his crouch and ran to another tree. The explosion of light from the muzzle gave away McCourty's position. Remus locked his eyes on the location so he could call the shots. Another flash of light and a torrent of lead whistled through the forest. A high-pitched shriek responded as one of the monsters took the bullet that sailed. The noise pierced his ears, making the gunfire sound like delicate church bells in comparison.

Skunk begged for help back and to his left. Remus ignored the large man's calls as he looked to save his own neck. The fright wriggled down his spine. Remus scampered to the section of brush where McCourty had been hunkered down. He smacked into the sharpshooter, knocking the gun from his hands.

"The hell?" McCourty swore as the sudden invasion of his personal space scared him and rid his fists of their only chance of survival. He shimmied forward on hands and knees, feeling along the turf for his weapon. Remus heard the tap of long fingernails against the wooden stock. Relief washed over him, happy that McCourty had recovered the rifle.

"Shoot. Shoot. Shoot." Remus stamped his hat down and braced for the concussion of forty-four caliber bullets. McCourty levered another round into the chamber. He knelt on his right knee and took aim.

A wall of meat and hair bowled over McCourty like a train barreling across the tracks. In one blink, Remus saw McCourty in front of him. And then he was gone.

Skunk's torment took a back seat to the more urgent screams of McCourty. The sharpshooter blubbered like a small child who had lost their toy. His screams dovetailed into begging and after a splashy ripping noise the man's voice cut out. Remus hyperventilated.

He waited an eternity as the nearby silence twisted his throat closed. Skunk's shouts faded into the background. A thud hit the ground before Remus and he watched the fern leaves roll towards him like an oncoming wave. Something stopped at his feet. Remus bent to inspect what had rolled to him.

McCourty's lifeless eyes stared up at Remus. His head, removed from his body, demanded all fibers of Remus' being. He screamed. Doing his best to step over the lost head, Remus ran as fast as he could. More thundering foot patter came at him. He felt it from the ground up. A long limb tripped him up. Remus struck the dirt hard, rolling over with the limb caught between his legs. After his body came to a stop, Remus reached down and pushed the limb out of his way. The sensation of a severed leg shook him to his core. Remus thought he had tripped on a leg. Instead he had tripped on a leg. His hand retracted with a wet sheen of blood dripping from his fingers.

Remus screamed once again and hurried towards the river. He hoped to get taken downstream so the current could do most of the work. And the water might provide cover from the monsters that owned the forest. Skunk flew into Remus from behind. Both men somersaulted onto the bank of the river. Skunk, with one eye swollen shut and a mouth missing many teeth, clutched Remus by the shoulders. He begged incoherently, blood spraying from his torn mouth.

Wasting no time, Remus slapped Skunk hard and used his shoulder to launch Skunk into the river. Remus dove in after him, the icy water draining his fear and revitalizing his will to live. His head broke the surface as his arms began swimming his way with the current. Skunk gurgled in the slight rapids ahead of him. Remus swam quickly to catch his foreman before the man drowned.

The attack continued as rocks and wood sailed at them from the shoreline. The pummeling continued as if there had been an endless supply of items to hurl. All the while, the monstrous screams and crashing forest followed them down the river. After a barrage that lasted ten minutes or more, forcing the men to dunk their heads under water to protect their skulls, the attack petered out.

Remus held onto Skunk as they floated away. Skunk had passed out or died, neither of which Remus could tell in their condition. But he wedged Skunk's chin under the crook of his arm all the same. If Skunk lived, Remus would still need him to run the mine. And he could not bear to be alone in the horrific redwoods. Remus preferred to hang on to a dead man rather than travel by himself.

The pain that hurt Remus more than his bodily aches and bruises was the loss of his switch. The weapon he had crafted with his own hands and had worked into deadly perfection over years had been left behind in the forest of giant monsters.

Chapter Twenty-nine

James came to. Dazed and lost, he remained prone for the better part of an hour. The forest slumbered around him. The serenity was a direct contrast to the battle zone he had been privy to last time he had been on his feet.

He rolled onto his elbow, wincing from the dull ache in his arm but mostly from the sharp, piercing pain in his ribs. James tried to remember the last time he had felt so terrible. He had been thrown from horses, had fought a bear, been thumped by demons and ghosts, and worked the family farm. James grimaced at the realization as soon as he compared his notes.

Never.

His head throbbed and the back of his neck made a crunching sound as he rotated his skull upon his shoulders. James thought it couldn't be good to hear noises like that inside your body. He sat up and stretched forward towards his boots as far as he could without separating his spine from his hips.

Everything hurt.

James thanked God he had survived. The battle was far from over. James still needed to find Carson and rescue him from the wild men. He had to save Lok from Remus if it wasn't too late. And somehow, get back to the mine to repay Remus Phillips and get some gold for his troubles. Taking some ore would be the only payment he could expect at this point.

Using every shaft of wood within reach, James pulled himself up. He shuffled across the undergrowth, catching his boot heels on every vine and rock hidden from view. Without energy, James could barely lift his toes with each step. The woods remained treacherous even lacking the wild men and Remus. James found a piece of timber as tall as he was, and as thick around as post hole digger. He used the wood as a walking stick, jabbing the earth ahead to direct his steps. It helped to hold his weight upright too. With his free hand, James clutched at his ribcage as if he had to hold his insides together.

He gingerly stepped along the game trail, following the worn path towards the river's edge. Slipping through overgrown branches and briars, James cared little for treading quietly. Until he heard movement from his right. The noise startled him. James froze in place. He held his breath and listened. The sound had been faint but close. He dismissed it for some small game. James sauntered on. Then he caught movement out of the corner of his eye. The shape much too small to be one of the beasts. It looked like a small person. James' heart pounded in his chest.

"Carson?"

The movement ceased. James leaned forward, hoping to make out the shape again as it collapsed amongst the background.

"Is that you, Carson?"

"James?"

James jumped. The weakened voice surprised him even after finding a person in his vicinity. The pronunciation of his name revealed the interloper.

Lok Lee.

"Lok? Where are you?" James held the walking stick in front of his chest as a precaution.

The smaller man emerged from the shadows. The forest remained too dark to make out his features but James could tell by the size and the general appearance of the clothing that he had indeed found Lok.

"Lok here. Lok hurt."

James attempted to throw his arm around Lok in an embrace. But both men grumbled and hissed, pain ailing them at once. James took a deep breath, glad to be with someone he counted as an ally.

"Where's Remus and Skunk? Are they alive?"

Lok explained how they had left him for dead and he pretended to be just that so they would go without more torture. He didn't know where they were or if they lived. Lok had hidden in place until he had heard James coming closer. He had hoped to get rescued by another miner but he was much happier it had been James.

James felt the same. The only missing piece of the puzzle was Carson. James checked Lok's injuries in preparation of their travels. Lok sustained more superficial injuries compared to James. He had cuts and bruises. Still nothing to shrug off but James had potentially fractured bones and he wondered if he would ever walk the same again.

Lok held the walking stick from the right side, his hand lower on the timber than James'. The synchronized their steps so they could utilize the wood as a guide, and as a weapon if needed. James inquired if Lok had gotten any information from Remus and Skunk as to where Carson had gone. Lok relayed that all Remus cared about was finding James and killing him.

James chuckled to himself. He would be ready for Remus when the time came. It wouldn't matter how hurt he was, James had a debt to pay and he would see it satisfied.

"Lok no work. Lok no pay."

James pursed his lips. He had ruined Lok's earning potential and nearly got him killed. James was glad Lok was alive. But he had to make up for so much damage. And he promised again to get Lok home to his family. Somehow James would get it done. He kept his promises to himself so as not to give false hopes to Lok.

"Let's take a break. My back hurts really bad." James tilted the walking stick down so he could slide off it onto a boulder that sat nestled between two redwoods. Relief in his feet and legs quickly turned to sharp pain up his spine and neck. James grimaced and breathed heavily until the white lights behind his eyes faded, signaling a settling of his anguish.

Lok sat against James, his shoulder providing another cushion to lean on. James felt his stomach gurgle. The hunger pangs rolled through his shirt. Lok laughed as he heard the noise.

"Lok hungry too. Lok no eat."

James rolled his neck and lifted himself to his feet. "Yeah, no sense sitting around when we have to cover a lot of ground on empty bellies." He stepped back into the trail with Lok attached to his walking stick. The walking wounded pair silently moved on, with no food to fill their stomachs. And much on their minds.

Chapter Thirty

The wild man's pace slackened. Carson thought they would stop to take another pee break. He felt like they had relieved themselves only a short while ago. Carson's bladder was fine but he assumed the wild man required more trips to the weeds than a human.

THEY ARE HERE.

Carson craned his neck as if stretching higher than he sat would clarify who the wild man referenced. He heard rustling ahead. However, the night continued to shadow the forest, making it impossible to see beyond a foot or two.

The wild man halted. Carson almost lost his balance. He clutched a fistful of stringy hair to hold on.

OUCH. YOU ARE PULLING MY HAIR.

Carson apologized inside his mind. He kept quiet so he could find out who they had come across. Besides the rustling, Carson heard whispers. The words were unbelievably soft but robust enough that Carson could recognize human language. His breath caught in his throat. He hoped it was someone who could take him back to James.

The wild man stooped, cradling Carson from his shoulder and placing him gently among the brush along the trail. His massive frame rose to its full stature, towering above like the trees throughout the forest.

"Who is it?" Carson spoke a bit louder than he had intended.

YOUR PEOPLE. THEY ARE AFRAID.

Carson took several more steps. He rested his hands on his knees, peering into the dense foliage.

TELL THEM THEY ARE SAFE.

Carson cleared his throat. He hesitated. The people could jump out and hurt them. They pretended to be afraid just so they could trick Carson and the wild man.

"He won't hurted you. It's okay." Carson rubbed his nose as a long strand of stray hair had wandered from his hat to his face.

"Carson?"

"James?"

Carson almost collapsed. His blood swelled and filled his heart with joy. He hopped in the air. His boots nearly slid off his feet.

"Carson!" Two men emerged from the dark. Their movements troubled Carson. A tad off-kilter and slow, James and Lok moved closer. Carson dove into James' arms. He clasped his hands behind James' neck and pulled him tight. James groaned. He hugged Carson in return but without the strength Carson had been used to.

"Easy there, fella. I'm a bit broke up." James held Carson's face in both his hands. He felt along Carson's arms and torso checking for all the parts. "Am I grateful to see you again, buddy. I thought those monsters took you away to," James didn't finish his sentence. His expression faltered and he shoved Carson behind his back, protecting him from the thing that hovered over them.

"Run Carson. I'll be right behind you." James pushed Carson with one hand behind his back.

"I don't wanted to run. I'm tired."

Carson tugged on James' shirt.

James swung the walking stick at the wild man's knees. The wood snapped in half with splinters flying in every direction. The creature barely flinched. A meaty hand swatted James into the grass.

"He won't hurted you. I told you." Carson moved in front of James. He threw his hands in his friend's face to stop him from charging. "He's my friend."

James lumbered to his feet. He glared at the wild man, fists clenched and ready for battle.

The giant growled, forcing everyone to deal with the tingling in their organs. James grasped his chest and stepped closer to the monster.

"They ain't no friends of ours. Your friend tried to kill me a few hours ago. He hurt me really bad, Carson. And I aim to give him what he came for."

GIVE HIM THE MESSAGE.

Carson jumped. He had been so focused on James that the voice in his heard scared him half to death.

"He wants to be left alone. He wants to live like we do."

James spat. "Oh, I bet he does. Why don't we just make him a huge bed and give him his own room. Better yet, let's give him a gun and see how he shoots." James felt around for another stick for a weapon.

ALL WHITE MEN ARE THE SAME. TELL HIM.

Carson rubbed his temples. His head started to ache from the loud words in his mind. Carson grew angry with the wild man's insistence and the hard-headedness of James.

"Pay attention, James. He doesn't wanted to make trouble. They're friends. I like them."

James laughed. "Them? You LIKE them?" He slapped Lok's arm as he pointed from Carson to the beast. "He likes them, Lok."

Lok stared up at the hairy face. He stood motionless as if James hadn't addressed him.

"If he's so friendly, Carson, then why did they rip apart the camp? How come they snatched you up and ran off? Why did they beat the crap outta me? Huh? What kind of friend does that?" James' breathing grew more erratic. Carson had seen James whip himself into a fury before a fight. And it always started with the heavy breathing.

GOODBYE. I WILL LEAVE NOW SO YOU CAN GO HOME.

"No." Carson shouted. He spun and clutched at the hairy stalks. The blubbering overflowed as his frustrations became too much to handle. "Don't go. You can beed our friend."

"Carson."

The aggression in his best friend's voice pushed him over the edge.

"Shut up, James. Shut up. I nevered haved a friend before. He's mine."

The words shot James through the heart. His shoulders sagged and his breathing shallowed. James glanced at his feet.

"Mine. My friend. You can't stopped me." Carson screamed as the flood gates opened. A bubble of spit popped from the corner of his mouth. His crying had forced his chest to heave and shudder. The wild man bent to console Carson. A massive hand enveloped his entire back and gently patted him. Carson fell into the warm, fuzzy embrace of the wild man. His heart ached because he had found himself in a bad situation. His best friend in the entire world wouldn't accept his new friend. And Carson had become quickly attached to the family of the forest.

He shook and pouted. His lower lip got sucked into his mouth by the fury of his wailing. Carson peered at James through a clump of hair. He tried to figure out how to convince James to accept his new friends.

Chapter Thirty-one

The river calmed where the terrain flattened out. Remus had pulled himself onto the sandy shore, soaked to his innards and exhausted from the long night. He dragged Skunk until the large man touched bottom. Then he left him to make his own way to land. It had been hard enough keeping Skunk's head above water.

Remus shook the drops from his red hair like a dog. He plopped onto his back; arms outstretched. The new day's sun crested the mountains. He silently begged for the sun to rise higher so it could dry him off. Remus slowed his breathing as his body tingled with delight with rest.

Skunk stomped his way onto shore, making loud squishy noises inside his boots. The man's wild mane sagged under the weight of the waterlogging. He collapsed a few feet from Remus, gasping like he had run several miles. Remus grew more irritated with each breath. He rolled onto his side and glowered at his foreman.

"Be quiet. I'm the one who should be out of breath. All you did was lumber all over me like a dead log." He cupped a handful of sand and threw it at Skunk. Then he dropped to his back again.

Skunk brushed the sand away from his clothing, mostly unsuccessfully as each grain stuck to the soggy fibers. He scooped a handful of soil and flung it directly at Remus. The dirt slapped Remus' face. He sat up, crunching grit in his teeth, and swabbing the filth from his eyelids.

"You bastard." Remus climbed onto unsteady legs. His eyes burned from the grains that had infiltrated his sockets. The right hand grabbed at his side where his trusty switch should have been. Remus cursed his luck and charged Skunk.

The large man had only climbed to his knees by the time Remus shouldered into him. Skunk hardly tilted. Remus took the brunt of his own velocity, bouncing off Skunk like child's ball. Skunk rose, lifted Remus by his throat and slapped him across the face. Remus flew backwards. A rosy handprint took form along his jaw. Eyes watered and filled with hatred, Remus went at Skunk once more. He feinted a right hook but caught Skunk in the nose with left jab as the foreman ducked into the punch.

Skunk faltered but kept his feet.

"I should kill you like the rotten yard dog you are." Remus raised his fists and circled Skunk.

"You can try but I wouldn't bet on your chances." Skunk swiped the blood that rushed from his busted nose. He followed Remus' steps without his hands up to defend.

Remus cursed again that he had lost his whip. He knew he could punish Skunk into submission with the razor-sharp tip of his weapon. With only his bare hands, Remus had to agree with his foreman's conclusions. Skunk was a behemoth. Massive and strong as multiple bulls.

"You're right." Remus lowered his fists. He sighed. "You are the only man in this whole outfit I can trust. Sometimes I forget how valuable you are to me."

He stretched his hand to Skunk.

"I apologize. Truce?"

Skunk huffed. He licked away some of the spatter that covered his lips. The large man stepped forward to accept Remus' hand.

Remus clutched Skunk's fist like a baby's hand inside a bear's paw and smashed his forehead into Skunk's face. The foreman howled in pain, flopping to the ground with his blood pouring between his fingers.

"But don't you forget who the man is. I'M the man." Remus kicked more sand at Skunk. He rounded the downed man, taunting him at every turn. "If you had done what I told you to, we would never have been in trouble. All you had to die was tie the damn guy up." Remus kicked at Skunk's ribs, connecting with a horrific thud. Skunk dropped down lower but kept his hands at his gushing face.

Remus stared at the high ridges, gathering his breath. The adrenaline shook his extremities as he mentally celebrated his victory over Skunk. Even without his switch, Remus had been the man to beat. And he remained undefeated.

Approaching Skunk, Remus prepared to gloat over his opponent when the foreman squeezed his ankle and tossed Remus aside. Before he could recover, Skunk climbed over Remus' back. He wrapped his meaty arm under Remus' chin and crushed the man's windpipe into the crook of his shoulder. Remus dug his fingernails into Skunk's skin. He drew blood but the large man only tightened his grip. Remus stretched his left hand over his head and attempted to push his thumb into Skunk's left eye. The big man leaned backwards, adding distance from Remus, and crushing his windpipe harder.

Remus watched the darkness cloud the edges of his vision. His tongue darted out, lapping at air like a cat would a saucer of milk. His ears had been muffled by Skunk's arm but he hung on each word as if it were his lifeline.

"Take your medicine, you mean little man. You will never push me around again. Never." Skunk's nose bled all over the back of Remus' head. "I've always hated you but I have kept my mouth shut out of respect for your father. How could such a wholesome man have sired a devil's spawn?"

Remus started to black out.

"Pushing men around is one thing. But killing kids and little people like Lok? You are a coward. A coward."

Remus dropped his arms. His struggle had gotten him nowhere. He decided to give up this fight and take revenge on Skunk when the circumstance was more favorable. Remus repeated each word Skunk uttered so he could call upon them when his moment came. The realization that Skunk had been loyal to his dreadful father all these years instead of him hurt more than any physical abuse he could endure. Remus had believed his men had hung on his commands because they respected and feared him.

He was livid.

And he began planning his revenge even as his mind faded to unconsciousness.

James and Lok had been eliminated.

Now it would be Skunk's turn.

Chapter Thirty-two

James sighed. He started to reach for Carson, to console him. The hairy man towered over James even as he had bent to embrace Carson. James could do little in his condition. Even healthy, James knew the force these creatures could summon. He believed humanity to be powerless against this species.

Didn't mean he liked them though.

Waving his hands at the giant, James implored the wild man to release his little friend. The creature turned Carson towards James and stepped back. James smiled at Carson. His heart warmed whenever he took in the boy's cute, moody expressions. He crouched in front of Carson.

"Look, I almost died. I can't just forget what happened to me." He shot a dirty look at the wild man. A blank stare is all he got in return.

"You lefted me. How come you didn't come finded me? I was ascared."

James wrinkled his lips. "I tried. Remus tied me up. I escaped thanks to Lok." James nodded in the Chinaman's direction. "You were nowhere to be found. And then the wild men gave me what for."

Carson kicked at the ground. He sniffled and wiped his eyes on his shirt sleeve.

"They need our help, James."

He shook his head in disbelief. "We're the ones who need help, Carson. We came all this way from home. Found a great opportunity to make money. A fortune." James removed his hat and ran his fingers through the knotted hair. "Now we're stuck out here with no job and no supplies. How are we supposed to help THEM?"

"They want us to telled the message."

"What message? You keep talking about messages." James swung his arms in exaggeration as if he were plucking words from the ether.

"White men should leaved them alone so they lived free." Carson tugged James' shirt. "Like us, James. Family like us."

James glanced at Lok who shrugged. The wild man grumbled, a low guttural noise. James flinched at the perceived implications of the sound. He figured the creature grew weary of their arguing.

"Who are we supposed to talk to, Carson? Because the only folks in this place are the miners and they don't wanna hear nothing from us anymore." James pointed at the wild man. "Ain't you got anything better to do than push around a little kid?"

Carson punched James in the groin. James fell to his knees, clutching the last part of his body that had not been bruised or beaten - until now. He glowered at Carson.

"What's the big idea?" The question came forth in bursts as he choked for air. James never understood how he lost his wind when he took a shot in the nuts. The lungs were nowhere near his manly region.

Carson hooked one thumb over his shoulder at the wild man while pointing in James' upturned face. "He loved me. Taked care of me and learned me things. Please, James. They're friends."

James nodded. He found it increasingly more difficult to argue with Carson. The boy got smarter as he aged. And the wild man HAD brought Carson back. The boy looked no worse for the wear since he had been snatched away. But that was the part that still irked James. How come they stole Carson to begin with?

"Just answer this, Carson. If they are so friendly to you, then why did they kidnap you? Friends don't treat friends like that."

CHAPTER 32

Carson lifted his head as if he listened to a distant bird singing in the trees. He shrugged. "I tolded you he talked in my head. He tolded me I was special. That's why he talked to me."

James coughed, his hand cupping his manhood. He used Carson's shoulder to pull himself to his feet. James had forgotten all about the cryptic warnings Carson had raised. James had ignored it as childish nightmares or an overactive imagination. But Carson had been forthcoming. And the boy looked healthy and well. The wild men treated Carson better than they did the mining camp.

He asked for clarification about the attack on the company. Carson relayed a long-winded tale about their family fleeing from Indians and white men who tried to kill them off. Left with fewer options, the wild men chose to defend their loved ones and carve out a safe territory for them to live undisturbed. James listened, understanding the evil that infested his people. Carson and he had dreamed of battling bad guys since they were young. There was no lack of evil in the world and the boys had encountered it in every town. James believed the stories but he still could not fathom how to impart the request to others.

"Well, I guess they would have hurt you by now if they meant to do harm." James extended his hand above his head. The wild man remained still, not recognizing the sign of peace through a handshake. James wrinkled his brow and waved instead. "Thank you for looking out for Carson."

Silence spread between them as Carson and the wild man stared at each other.

"He said you are welcome and he thanks you for helping his people." Carson hugged James. His arms squeezed the sore ribs, forcing James to wince. James did his best to ignore the pain and hug Carson back.

"I'm hungry. We should find something to eat before we head back to the mine. Are you hungry?"

"Lok hungry. Lok eat."

Carson jumped up and down. "We eated bugs and they were yummied. Let's find ants."

James scratched his chin. He had no intention of eating insects and he started to wonder if Carson told long tales again.

"He said he will fixed us breakfast. Oh, boy. Wait till you taste it, James."

Lok rubbed his belly like Carson. The wild man stomped to the east, heading towards the river. James began conjuring lies to get out of eating anything strange. Carson and Lok followed the wild man, already far behind the creature's pace.

James slumped to his haunches. His belly growled and worked up some fresh saliva on the back of his tongue. Just the idea of eating a meal got his juices flowing. He snickered aloud and agreed that he was starving so much, he would consider eating bugs.

Chapter Thirty-three

Sour grapes would be an understatement. Remus walked in silence. He preferred not to speak at all after his fight with Skunk. The men hiked through the woods for several hours. Sounds of sifters and men laboring echoed from the forest ahead. Remus exhaled deeply, relieved the journey neared the end.

He had awakened in the spot where Skunk had bested him. While he was out cold, Remus' clothes had mostly dried and the respite preformed wonders on his mind and body. Lack of sleep and the intensity of the hunt had worn him down. He managed to fight through it and the best thing that had happened was getting a few hours of rest. Albeit not the type of rest he had hoped to find.

Remus vowed to repay Skunk in spades the first chance he got. When the time arrived, Remus would make an example of Skunk. The whole company would watch him bring the hulking man to his knees, begging for mercy. It would serve two purposes - re-establishing his absolute authority of the miners and it would help to quell any insurrection should Skunk be foolish enough to brag about his victory. Remus believed Skunk to be more of a man than a boastful idiot.

They would have to wait and see.

Rounding a copse of trees, the camp came into view. Tents had been resurrected in a smaller conglomeration, nearer the mine shaft. Safety in numbers appeared to win over as the men steered away from the woods.

Bustling activity continued in their absence, pleasing Remus. He rubbed his hands together and scoured the sifters as he closed in. Several men nodded in his direction but worked unabated. Dusty hurried down the slope from the mine. He waved his hat.

"Good to see you well, sir."

Remus ignored Dusty. He inspected a couple of chunks in his palms. Then tossed them back into the sifter. Skunk continued, returning inside the mine without a word. Remus smirked, happy to avoid an immediate scene.

"Didja find them, sir?" Dusty slapped his hat on his head. He cracked his knuckles and stared at Remus as the boss walked along the line of sifters.

"Won't be seeing James Johnson again." He soured when he watched Dusty's expression sag. "Took care of business. That's all."

Dusty craned his neck. He looked behind Remus and then shot a glance at the mine. "I ain't seen McCourty. Did I miss him?"

Remus clutched at the switch that no longer rested at his side. His fingers curled, frustrated he could no longer leverage the threat of a whipping. "McCourty didn't make it. Lost him to the monsters that invaded us the other night."

Dusty removed his hat and held it across his heart. He bowed his head and apologized for the loss. He said, "Good man, good man."

Remus groused. "Enough about McCourty. How are we on the schedule? Have you gotten us back on track as I expected?" He leaned into Dusty's personal space, increasing the man's discomfort. Dusty backed up a step.

"Uh, well, sir, we done as much as we could. What with the lost hands and all."

"Yes or no?" Remus shouted, drawing attention from the men who worked the sifters. Two miners who had emptied their payloads hurried their pace to disappear inside the mine before their numbers were called. "It's a simple question."

Dusty's throat bobbed as he worked up courage to provide the bad news. Remus began to feel at home again. Dominating his crew made him feel important. And it was what his father paid him for. To drive production. Any way necessary.

"Almost, sir." Dusty held up his finger and thumb to display a small measure of missing the mark. "I done like you said. The men have worked twenty hours each day and they only eat when the work is done." Dusty spoke out of the side of his lips, head slightly turned to keep the men from overhearing him. "I don't know how much longer I can keep pushing them, sir. Rumbles of mutiny all around. They're tired and hungry and ain't been paid."

Remus clenched his jaw. He snatched Dusty's collars and tugged the man closer. He raised his voice to hammer his authority home for those witnessing, and especially for those who would hear it through the grapevine.

"If this crew can't get the job done then I will find real men who can. I got crews of Chinks and Mexi-cans en route as we speak. And they work harder for longer hours and less pay." He spied a few miners milling about behind Dusty as they eavesdropped. "Everyone can be replaced. Remus shoved Dusty backwards. "Even you."

Dusty picked his hat up off the ground. He mumbled, "Yes, sir," then ran for the mine. Remus glowered at the men within sight. He stepped in their general direction and a grin escaped his lips as the miners made haste for their work.

Content with his "homecoming," Remus decided to tear through the tunnels. He would check on the progress with his own eyes to kick the activity into a second wind. And he would stem the chatter as nobody would wish to be caught talking about him behind his back. Remus helped himself to some hard tack from the chuck box. He leaned against the stand, reinforcing his will over everyone. Satisfied with some food in his belly, Remus made his way towards the mine. He found a sizable stick on the edge of the brush. Remus hefted it to measure its weight in his hands. He needed a replacement for the switch and a big stick could fill in nicely. The wood required work to smooth out the knots and strip away the bark. He examined each end, imagining sharpening them to points that could be used for poking. And stabbing.

He tossed the stick into the grass. The beauty of the switch was its ability to withstand much abuse without breaking. The stick could break in half if he were not careful to use one solid enough for the job. Remus swore he would create the next tool for maximizing his management skills. It would come in handy with Skunk, too.

Chapter Thirty-four

With stomachs full of nourishment, the band of friends set off for the mining camp. Carson had clapped and laughed as he watched Lok and James dig into their meals. The wild man had concocted a different sandwich of sorts for everyone. Heaping portions of trout wrapped in large, crunchy leaves with tree sap drizzled over the top. And a generous helping of red ants, yanked from an overflowing ant hill. Carson took delight when the insects scurried from James' mouth like they had for him. James made faces and chewed quickly as if he wanted to get the meal over with. Lok hadn't batted an eye. He devoured his food without question.

James eventually enjoyed the breakfast. The squirming lips and fast-blinking eyes ceased. Carson thought he had even heard James moan with satisfaction as he ate. The wild man laughed as they shoved the trout into their mouths and burped.

WE'LL MAKE WILD MEN OF THEM YET.

Carson nodded as the voice filled his head.

James rehashed his discovery of Lok's treatment. He explained his intentions of retribution against Remus. As James expelled his frustrations, Carson imagined the wild men storming the encampment again. This time he hoped they would crush the men that done James harm.

THAT DEFEATS THE PURPOSE.

Carson jumped. He forgot his mind was open to others. He questioned the wild man.

THE MESSAGE. IF WE DESTROY THEM THEN HOW WILL THEY UNDERSTAND OUR WISHES?

The voice vibrated his skull. Carson itched behind his ears. He imagined Mobay being attacked by the miners. His heart thumped with pain as such pictures hurt him just to think about his friend getting abused.

The wild man grunted.

YOU ARE WISE BEYOND YOUR YEARS.

Carson asked the wild man for guidance. His rage caused him to tap his foot uncontrollably. Carson wished he could punch Remus or hit him in the head with a gun grip like he had seen James do countless times. He tried to understand these new feelings of hostility. Carson had been free from unbridled anger his whole life. But now he wanted to act upon these new impulses and protect his loved ones the way they had protected him.

I AM SAD FOR YOU, CARSON.

The wild man patted Carson's back like a father consoling a boy over a deceased dog. Carson looked up into the dark eyes. He interpreted deep concern etched within the coal orbs.

A CHILD IS INNOCENT. THAT IS WHAT DREW ME TO YOU. INNOCENCE IS LOST WHEN A BOY BECOMES A MAN.

Carson shook his head. He didn't believe himself to be a man. Hair had not grown along his cheeks yet. And his voice sounded like a woman. Carson traced his arms for hidden muscles, wondering if he had missed the transition to manhood. The wild man chuckled.

MANHOOD HAS NOTHING TO DO WITH YOUR BODY. IT IS YOUR SPIRIT.

James droned on about challenging Skunk too. Lok nodded as he prattled on.

MEN ARE PRONE TO VIOLENCE AND GREED. MEN BELIEVE IN DEBTS. AND DEBTS REQUIRE PAYMENT. A BOY CARES LITTLE FOR THESE THINGS. A BOY DOES NOT KNOW THESE CONCEPTS.

CHAPTER 34

Carson blinked away the rush of tears. He hadn't realized the threshold had been crossed from one world to the next. His memories flooded by, times laughing and running through the fields. Waking to each new day like it was a fresh adventure of fun and stimulation. Only concerned with happiness and following James, his hero and idol. The heaviness of revenge weighed him down. Carson sagged into the log. A cold sweat beaded along his neck. He felt scared. How could he be a man? He wasn't finished being a boy. If he were a man then he would have to be serious and working alongside James would be more like a job. A real job.

DO NOT RUSH FORWARD. THERE WILL BE TIME ENOUGH FOR THOSE THINGS. RECONSIDER YOUR FEELINGS.

Carson rubbed his boot across the dirt, erasing the prints like he wished to whisk away his new thoughts.

"Once I get inside the mine, I can convince the men to stand up to his tyranny." James stood and patted his hat against his leg to release the dustiness.

"Lok help. Lok scared." The small man followed James' lead.

"What are we doing, James?" Carson grabbed James' arm as he began to head up the trail.

"I just told you, Carson. Haven't you been listening to me this whole time?" James crossed his arms.

Carson shook his head. "No."

James sighed. "I'll explain it again while we walk. We don't have time to waste. Let's go."

Carson refused to move. James and Lok continued for twenty yards until they realized Carson hadn't followed. James hurried back, his boots kicking up dirt with each frustrated stomp.

"We need to go. Now."

Carson shook James' hands off his shoulders. He spun to face the wild man. A blank expression greeted him, leaving Carson with his own decision to make.

"I'm in charged, James. Not you."

"Carson, we ain't got time for your games. I know what I'm doing and you're just a kid."

The wild man stood over James. He grabbed James' shirt and lifted him several feet above the ground. The bass grumbling rattled the hat right off James' head. His eyes bugged beyond the sockets as fought to escape the hairy man's grasp.

Carson asked him to put James down. The wild man complied, listening to Carson's internal command.

"You should have paid attention, James." Carson grinned and brushed past James on his way up the trail. The wild man thumped along behind Carson. Lok shrugged and giggled as he followed the other two. James, jaw agape, remained behind.

"What the hell just happened?"

He scurried to catch up once the group disappeared along the tree line. Carson glanced over his shoulder, pleased to find everyone falling in line.

I HOPE YOU KNOW WHAT YOU ARE DOING.

Carson picked a leaf off a branch and ripped little sections off, tossing them as he walked. I do, he thought. This time I'll show James that I'm not a kid anymore. I'm a man.

The wild man laughed and cautioned Carson.

WALK BEFORE YOU RUN, LITTLE ONE.

Chapter Thirty-five

The sifters clunked and chugged through tons of soil. With less men to work the mine, the business of sifting had slowed until the miners had been redeployed. Fewer mined while more worked the sifting end to uncover gold enough to hit the company's target goal.

James stooped behind a boulder near the entrance to the mine. He scouted the camp. The circle of tents had drawn closer and nearer the mine. A new fire pit had been built within the center of the tents. He counted the number of shelters to estimate how many men had survived the wild man attack.

Skunk trod from the darkness in the shaft. James slid down, surprised by the man's sudden arrival. He grabbed a small stone, raised up over the boulder and threw it at the back of the large man. James ducked before he heard the thump of the rock connecting with its target. He tip-toed as quietly as he could along the side of the hill but the leaves and detritus crinkled beneath his feet.

James flattened his back along the mine, hoping to get the jump on Skunk. As the man rounded into view, James caught Skunk's jaw with a right hook. Skunk toppled to his back, stunned by the punch. James followed his momentum and straddled the behemoth. He clutched Skunk's collars and slammed his head into the ground twice.

Skunk's eyes rolled around.

"I'm gonna make you pay. You hear me?" James whispered, his mouth close to Skunk's ear.

The large man shook his head. The wild gray and black mane swayed as Skunk cleared the cobwebs from the attack.

"James?" His voice barely audible.

James cocked his fist and prepared for another strike. "I figured you to be a decent man but I guess I had you pegged wrong."

Skunk blinked away the daze. "James. I thought you were dead."

"You mean you had hoped I was dead." James punched Skunk in the face. The strike echoed off the boulder like a woman had slapped an incorrigible man in a saloon. Skunk's head bounced off the ground. His nose bled.

"James. Stop." Skunk bucked his chest. James flew into the side of the mine headfirst. His hat flew off and his body crumpled in a heap. Before James could recover Skunk pushed all his weight into James, pinning him into the earthen wall along the mine shaft.

"Stop. Stop." Skunk's blood dripped into his mouth. James covered his face as he watched Skunk's eyes fade from crazed to calm. "What's gotten into you, boy?"

"You tortured Lok and you tried to kill me. Or did you forget what you did already?"

Skunk threw James to the ground. He dabbed at the blood in his mustache with the back of his hand. "I didn't do anything to Lok. YOU got that man killed when you ran off. Remus whipped me too for your stunt."

James gathered his wind. He used climbed to his feet, squaring off with Skunk. "You tricked us into thinking you cared about us. But your only friend is Remus."

Skunk smiled. The smile transformed into a chuckle. "I hate that man more than anyone I've ever known. And I've met some terrible folks in my day." Skunk spit out some blood and settled his back against a tree.

CHAPTER 35

James closed the distance. His fists clenched for more action. Skunk nodded at his approach.

"Put those things away. I am not going to fight you." Skunk checked his teeth, one by one. "And you should be glad of that because I would sweep the forest clean with the likes of you."

James released his fists. He put his hat on his head and crouched to take the strain out of his back and neck. The sharp pain returned after Skunk tossed him around.

"I saw you. Remus beat Lok and you did nothing."

"What was I to do? McCourty had a rifle and I knew he had more loyalty to that bastard than me. I did my best to convince him Lok and the search for you were a waste of time. But he only wanted blood."

James scanned Skunk for truth. "Then why are you still doing his bidding? Why not leave?"

"And go where, James? I am too old to start over with some other outfit. Mr. Phillips likes me. He entrusted me with watching out for his boy and running the miners like I was the boss man. Took me years to develop their respect and earn my promotions. I'm not going to throw it away because his son is a madman." Skunk came to James. He wrapped his muscles around James' neck. "I prefer to live with the devil I know. Gives me a chance to survive."

James melted under the man's touch. He wondered if his father's arm would feel the same if it coached him through life's intricacies. James thought about his daddy for the first time in a long time. His legacy is what spurred James to leave Texas and everywhere else.

Skunk queried James about his return to life. He was relieved to hear of Lok's survival and reuniting with Carson. James left out the parts about the wild man feeding them and helping them come back to the camp. What Skunk didn't know might protect him. For now.

"I'm gonna put a hurtin' on Remus. You can either help me or stay out of my way. But I ain't stopping until he gets what he deserves."

Skunk picked at flakes of bark along a tree. His head shook. "I don't think that's a good idea, James. You should count your blessings and head back where you come from while you still can. Remus is not like a bar brawler." Skunk poked James in the chest with a think finger. "That man is evil. Plain and simple."

James ignored the warning. He asked if Skunk could find his gun and knife. Skunk confirmed he had gathered both their belongings after he had tied James up. He wanted to protect the gear from the grubby hands of the miners who would pick through the leftovers before James had gotten a fair trial. James thanked Skunk and they conspired where Skunk would hide the stuff so James could retrieve it. He walked Skunk through his plans for confronting Remus. Skunk repeated his warnings but agreed to assist James in any way he could.

Chapter Thirty-six

He tapped his fingertip over the needle-like precision of his handicraft. A drop of blood rose to the surface, filling the whorls in his fingerprint. Remus grinned sheepishly. He raised the end to the sky, admiring the new weapon he had carved with his knife. Behind the tip of his spear, Remus caught Skunk returning to camp from the side of the mine.

Remus whistled. Skunk, like all the men at the sifters, had been drawn to the sound. Remus waved Skunk over. The sifters sighed with relief and busied themselves with their work. His pleasure amplified, seeing the men happy their number had not been called. Skunk weaved his way past the fire pit and tents. He paused before the stool Remus sat on.

"Sir."

Wishing to test out his new tool, Remus thought about jamming the point into Skunk's belly. Remus reined himself, savoring the possibility for becoming a reality later. "Where were you just now?"

Skunk shifted from left to right. His eyes darted along the forest. Remus sensed an untruth coming. "I was relieving myself." Remus rose. He stepped close enough to Skunk to force the big man to lean back.

"I haven't forgotten your behavior, by the way."

"Behavior?" Skunk wrinkled his forehead.

Remus inspected the fine point on his spear. He held the sharp end within inches of Skunk's face. "Yes. You wished to look out for the Chink and call of the search for James. Odd, considering what we knew to be the truth. Don't you think?"

Skunk pursed his lips. Remus smelled the fear wafting from the sweat that soaked Skunk's shirt.

"Didn't see it as a wise use of our time. We'd already fallen behind schedule."

"It doesn't matter what YOU see as a waste of time. What YOU think is not important at all. Your only job is to do I as tell you to. Was that not clear to you when we left Sacramento?"

Skunk opened his mouth to reply. Then closed it. Remus rolled the spear around in his palm so the point would spin in a tight circle before Skunk.

"When I lost my switch, I felt downtrodden. Like I had become a dog with no bark." Remus swung the spear around so the other sharpened point rose to the sky. He smiled as Skunk's eyes crossed at the extreme close-up of Remus' new toy. "So I fashioned this spear to provide voice where it had once been. Spears can bleed a man just as much as a switch, don't you think?"

Skunk nodded.

"Anyway, enough about my new friend. I'm worried about you, Skunk."

"Me? Why, sir?" Skunk almost toppled backwards as Remus edged closer.

"We had left the forest with an understanding about James and Lok. I'd hate to see you pricked by anything short of the truth. I've learned, over many years, that lies and rumors could cut a man very badly if he wasn't careful." Remus whispered into Skunk's left ear. "Have you been careful, Skunk?"

"Yes, sir. I have no need to speak to the men except to motivate them to work harder and faster." Skunk turned askew, leaving his back to Remus.

He used the tip of the spear to press gently into Skunk's back. Applying little pressure, Skunk stiffened at the sharpness.

CHAPTER 36

"So glad we are on the same page. Your loyalty might earn you another promotion in the future." Remus pressed harder. The tip dug into Skunk's flesh and a small circle of blood expanded from the center of the wound. "Disloyalty would be a major disappointment for all of us."

Skunk stepped away from the spear. He faced Remus with an expression that bordered on fear and mindlessness. Remus hardly cared which. He could tame the beast using either attribute.

"Unfortunately, for now, I have promoted Dusty to your position. And YOU will replace Dusty as an assistant. I trust the temporary demotion won't harm our working relationship. Now you will have an opportunity to prove your renewed dedication to the company. And it will keep you by my side so I can monitor your growth, personally." Remus grinned.

Skunk stared at the ground, nodding. Remus dismissed Skunk to work with the sifters and keep the line moving. Dusty would absorb the lion's share of the mining leadership. Skunk's shoulders slumped forward as he strode the line.

Remus sat down, whittling his blade along the spear's shaft. He etched a handy grip in the center, with notches for his fingers to hold on tight. He regretted not applying such detail to his switch now that it had been lost. Utilizing different implements had been a benefit for Remus through the years. Men knew how to fight with knives. And a gun would be too…final for controlling his men. The switch had brought fear and respect since most men knew little about fighting one with such a weapon. Before the switch, Remus had a branding iron. It, too, struck a chord with men as they feared being burned or bludgeoned with the iron. His father had taken the branding iron away after Remus brained a young man from Oklahoma. Remus never forgot the colors that leaked from the crack in the man's skull. Some of it had oozed from his ears too. A spear, as primitive as it seemed, would do well to throw off any notions of disrespect.

Nobody would be skilled to fend off the spear. And it added to his arsenal of motivators for getting what he needed out of his men.

Remus tried to fit the spear inside his switch loop but the spear slid out the bottom too easily. He looked about the camp for something to shrink the hole so he could free his hands until such a time that required the spear to come out. As he practiced pulling the spear free and walking about, Remus ground his teeth. The spear was too long to carry at his side. Even if he fixed the loop on his belt, he realized he would be challenged to walk comfortably, sit down, stand up and run. Remus caught himself before he tried to break the spear in half over his knee.

He thought about his trusty switch and wondered if he could send one or two of his men to find it and bring it back to him. Remus cursed himself for chasing James into the dreaded redwoods. It had cost him dearly.

Chapter Thirty-seven

Preparing for the attack involved many moving parts. Carson had taken charge of most of the details. He had assumed the lead role because his newfound masculine rage dictated his actions. Carson agreed to one of the proposals presented by James. Otherwise, the command rested in his hands.

He told the wild man to gather troops. Using various imitations of birds and forest critters, the wild man called out to his clan. Chirps and whistles signaled receipt of the message. Carson stared with awe at the wild man's range of vocals. He laughed at several calls because the wild man had to contort and make silly faces to achieve some of the vocalizations.

Within the hour, a frightening assembly of wild men hunkered around the small boy. He had been amazed by the variety of colors and sizes of the clan members. Most were extremely tall and muscular, with chiseled chests and biceps. If Carson hadn't communed with the wild man's family, he would have messed his britches at the sight of such massive creatures. The hair color varied from light brown with reddish hues to deep black. Even the length of hair differed. Some wild men had long, wispy hair like a woman would wear their hair down. Others had sparse patches of hair, short as a young boy straight from the barber's chair.

All had faces that resembled men.

A few of the odd creatures frightened Carson. There was an albino wild man with pinkish orbs tucked beneath a banana-colored brow. Its white palms matched its coat. Carson wondered if the albino one was special like him or if they came in all colors and this one had been the sole representative of the "whites." A stout, brown creature stood off to the right. He had none of the attributes of the rest of the wild men as his belly distended like an old, drunken barfly. His arms failed to reach his knees, reminding Carson of the slats in a water barrel, hugging close to the rounded middle. Even his head was shaped differently. Almost all wild men had a cone-shaped skull that titled backwards but the rotund member had a flattened skull as if he had fallen off a cliff and landed plum on his head. Carson nearly laughed in the wild man's face until he had been caught staring for too long. Lastly, one wild man looked like a strange bird. It was very skinny and long, with a smallish head and a misshapen face. The nose and lips jutted forward like a buzzard beak. Carson shivered as he imagined encountering the weird wild man alone in the wild.

WE ARE ALL GATHERED.

Carson startled. The voice echoed in his mind and ripped him from his inspection of the crowd surrounding him. The wild man acted as interpreter, reading Carson's thoughts on the plan of action. He relayed the plan through tongue clicks and chatter which Carson hadn't heard before. It was as if the wild man possessed another language for it differed from the communications with his wife and son. Carson stared, again amazed at the contortions and noises which escaped the thin lips of his friend. Creatures nodded or grunted as they internalized the commands being shared.

WE ARE READY FOR TONIGHT.

Carson hugged the wild man's leg. He fluttered his lips as a clump of hair accidentally tangled in his mouth. A chorus of laughter erupted around the circle as the wild men drifted into the forest. Carson shuddered as each creature appeared to collapse into the foliage like ghosts, disappearing as if they were fauna themselves. He wished he could cloak himself too. Carson imagined sneaking up on James and spooking his friend. Or stealing treats from a mercantile without the owner noticing him.

CHAPTER 37

The wild man said goodbye before he returned to his family. He warned Carson to take care not to get caught up in the fray. The wild man reminded him that James and Lok would be in danger of the attack as well because the creatures had not met them. Without their scents and facial recognition, the wild men were ready to pounce on the mining camp and Carson's friends might get caught up in the destruction. Carson nodded, thinking James and Lok would be smart enough to avoid being in harm's way.

FOR THEIR SAKES, LET'S HOPE YOU ARE RIGHT.

The wild man patted Carson's head and left the clearing.

Carson felt suddenly alone in the redwoods. He scanned the woods for danger, afraid he would be open to evil no that his massive gang of friends had departed. Carson scurried back to the trail which led to the encampment. He felt giddy with nervousness at having taken charge for the first time in his life. Only Civil War generals and Indian chiefs commanded armies. And now Carson imagined himself on par with the military greats. He pictured himself in paintings, talked about in classrooms across the west, sitting on a gallant steed and glaring into the distance while he planned his army's attack.

The sounds of the mining camp grew louder as Carson ducked through the underbrush to draw closer. He knelt in a soft patch of pine needles, peeking through the dense ferns. A dozen men worked the sifters, scraping and scratching at dirt and rock for miniscule flakes of gold. Skunk supervised the work, traveling the line back and forth, stopping periodically to poke his giant fingers into the trays.

Just beyond the sifters sat Remus Phillips. The redheaded ogre glared at his men from beneath bushy brows. His hands worked tirelessly on a stick, the sound of his sharp blade whittling the wood to a dangerous shape. Carson wished he could charge Remus and defeat the angry man, ending the fight before anyone could get hurt. He imagined punching the man in the face and headbutting his nose so hard that blood splattered the earth at his feet. Carson felt a surge of rage pump through his veins. His breathing quickened along with his heartbeat. Carson gripped the ferns, crumbling soft green petals in his hands.

He ducked quickly.

Remus had turned to look over his left shoulder in Carson's direction. He returned to his craft and watched the men work the sifters.

Carson backed away, afraid Remus had heard him or sensed his presence.

Chapter Thirty-eight

The plan almost failed before it started. James had waited far too long for Remus to leave his post. The man had perched upon his stool like a scarecrow in a field protecting the crops from magpies. With Remus so close to the center of camp, James could not risk his discovery or the surprise would be wasted. He chewed his dirty fingernails and spit the gritted scraps as he spied impatiently from the forest.

Once night fell, the fire pit cast gloomy shadows along the camp. The torchlight wavered over the sifters as the men leaned closer to the trays, squinting to see what they were doing.

Happy to have his pistol back on his hip and his knife at his side, James felt more confident about his chances of pulling off the plan to avenge his friends.

Remus finally rose and sauntered towards the mine. He barked orders at the miners toiling with the sifters. A pair of miners followed Remus into the darkened cavern. He led the way with one of the lanterns set upon the boulder near the mine entrance.

James darted past the tents, bent over and gliding on the tips of his boots to avoid creating too much noise. Most sounds would be drowned out by the continuous activity but he wanted to leave little to chance. He crouched behind the chuck box, peering over the top to see if he had been noticed. The miners worked without pause. James carefully lifted the lid and rooted around inside for perishables. He dug out an armload of jerky and two sacks of apples. Glancing about to ensure his escape, James took off for the wood line. He piled the sacks behind a grove of pines, pausing long enough to watch Lok gather the food and disappear deeper into the woods. They had set up a shallow pit to hide the food from critters until they could complete the mission.

He hurried back to the chuck box. As he slid down behind the crate, James had nodded at Skunk who had expected his maneuver. Skunk pretended not to spot the intrusion and he occupied the miners' attention with orders. James utilized the distraction to load up more jerky and hard tack. He pulled a burlap bag of beans or grains from the box and jammed the loose food stuffs inside to simplify his booty. James gently closed the lid and ran for the trees with his second load of goodies. Lok sat on his haunches, awaiting the following delivery. James swung the bag down, relieved to unburden his back with the hefty weight. Lok pulled the bag onto his shoulder like he lifted an airy rag, and the small man melted into the darkness beyond the pines. James shook his head at his friend's incredible strength.

Out of breath, James slouched behind the chuck box on his third trip. He gasped for wind and listened to the cadence of the work at the sifters. James peeked over the crate to make sure Remus remained absent. Satisfied the coast was clear, James dug through the box again. He stuffed his arms to overflowing with potatoes, corn and what felt like one hundred pounds of salted beef. He dropped a steak in the dirt as he drew closer to the forest. James left the meat behind so he could unfurl the heavy haul and rest his sore muscles. Again, Lok awaited the delivery. James grumbled under his breath. No sooner had he dumped the food on the ground, Lok had piled it back up and hurried into the darkness with it.

James rested with his hands on his knees. He realized he had held his breath the whole time, afraid to make noise. It only exasperated his struggle to steal the rations. He felt confident that most of the chuck box had been emptied. His fingers had traced some loose items in the bottom of the crate but James had taken the bulk of it. There wouldn't be enough to go around the camp for more than one meal or even a snack break. James gathered his dwindling energy and rushed to retrieve the steak he had dropped.

As he broke free of the woods, James saw Remus walking along the sifters with Skunk in tow. He threw himself to the dirt and kept his head down. Slowly, James raised his eyes to scan the camp. Luckily, he hadn't been discovered. But the steak sat like a thick lump in the middle of the expanse. James knew if he left it behind, Remus would follow the trail in their direction and they might recover the pilfered supplies. It was paramount that he get the steak out of sight or risk blowing up the whole arrangement.

James belly-crawled like a snake. He ignored the stems of weeds which tickled his nose as he shimmied close to the dirt. Remus straddled his stool. This time, the man faced James' direction as he warmed his hands over the fire. Using slow, tiny motions, James reached for the steak. His fingers scraped the side of the meat just beyond his reach. The risk would be too great to continue forward. James carefully felt along his side for his knife. Grasping the handle, James gently stabbed the side of the steak and lured it in his direction with calculated tenderness. With the steak under his nose, James bit into the beef with the knife still lodged in its side and pulled the meat backwards as he slithered into the underbrush. The juices and salts caused a flood of saliva to drool from his lips.

Safely behind the growth, James released his bite on the steak. He rubbed his sweaty forehead in the dirt and muddied the ground. James rolled to his back and stared at the canopy of branches above. He tried to slow his breathing by picturing his mother back on the farm. The memories did little to slow his breath with his emotions surfacing.

Lok tapped James' boot. He rose to find Lok pointing at the hunk of cured meat. James unplugged his knife and tossed the steak into Lok's open arms. The diminutive man hustled away with the beef while James stowed away his knife.

The rush of danger had revived his energy levels. But he knew he could do with less drama and worry. They still had so much to accomplish tonight. And this stressful beginning would only be the tip of the mountain.

Chapter Thirty-nine

Against his better judgment, Remus asked one of the men to prepare for supper. He instructed the man to ration out just one strip of jerky and one apple per miner. And he told the "volunteer" to put on a pot of coffee as a treat. They usually worked the mine until closer to midnight because of the slipping schedule. But Remus had tuckered himself out and he couldn't justify breaking for the night unless the company did as well.

The man hurried back to inform Remus that the food was gone. Remus spun on his heels. He lifted the lid and shined a lantern into the chuck box.

Scraps of cured meats and gnarled ears of corn or potatoes with sprouted eyes littered the bottom of the barren chest. His stomach churned. Remus slammed the lid closed. He clutched the man by the shirt and demanded to know what had happened to the supplies since the morning. The man shrugged and said he didn't know. Remus tossed the man aside. He would have bigger problems on his hands if he couldn't scrounge up some vittles for the men.

One by one the miners began to crowd around the fire. The grumbling grew louder as word spread about the missing rations. Remus grabbed his spear and walked a tight circle, thinking as fast as he could. He would send a hunting party to kill some meat but it would take too much time to get the animals, clean them and cook them for supper. Remus jammed one end of the spear into the ground, wishing he could stab it through a stack of fish.

Fishing would be quicker. He wondered how difficult it would be to score a dozen fish. The cleaning and cooking would be much faster than a deer or rabbits.

Men began to line up, five men deep. They drew in closer to the fire as their voices rose to a shrill cry for food. Remus glared at Skunk and Dusty along the back of the mob. Skunk shook his head. Remus waved Dusty over with a nervous finger. He grabbed Dusty's suspender and pulled him close so he could whisper above the din.

"The supplies have disappeared. Why wasn't someone guarding the food?"

"You wanted all hands on deck, sir." Dusty rubbed his beard. "Every able body has been digging or sifting, sir."

Remus gritted his teeth. He released Dusty's strap. "Find me something to pacify these men. If we don't fix this problem, we will have a mutiny on our hands."

Dusty nodded, straightened his chewed hat, and ran towards the back of the camp.

Remus dragged his stool to the middle, closer to the fire. He stepped up and peered along the angry faces in the crowd. Fists shook in the air and the noise grew to a deafening crescendo. Remus held the spear above his head, shaking it up and down as he shouted.

"Quiet. Quiet. QUIET." The cacophony petered out as the attention focused on their leader. Remus held his arms high, signaling the men to hold their tongues.

"You may have heard that we have a small problem."

"You're gonna have a problem, man." A faceless voice shouted from the mob. Remus glowered to find the brave soul but it was impossible to figure out who had spoken. The men cheered the words of the lone dissenter.

Remus waved his arms again. The noise softened.

"I am in the same position as you. I don't eat either. It's not like I have secreted bread to my tent."

"Let's check his quarters. I don't trust him one bit." The anonymous voice overstepped Remus. The mob worked into a lather once more. Men screaming and shaking knuckles at him. Remus begged Skunk to help, staring over the hostile faces. Skunk remained passive near the back. Remus clenched his fist. He would deal with Skunk later.

"I will figure this out. Trust me."

The miners began throwing their hats at Remus. Their shouts included cuss words and threats. The men complained they had been overworked and underfed. They demanded their back pay as all income had been withheld as an incentive for harder work and longer hours. The men were fed up and they needed blood to satisfy the pent-up frustration.

"Betcha can't whip us all at the same time, you thieving bastard."

Remus jumped off the stool. He used the spear as a prod and shoved a score of men backwards. He wanted to run them through with the sharp point but he needed the miners to finish the job. His mind blacked out when he pictured his father and the wretched, plumply built Romulus cornering him on why the expedition had failed. The anger bubbling to the surface overtook his senses. Remus pulled one of the miners to him and he jabbed the tip of the spear into the man's throat.

The crowd hissed and the mob backed up a few paces. Remus grinned through his clenched jaw.

"I can kill you all. One at a time, I can send you each to Hell with your tongues plucked from your mouths and your eyes carved out. Is that what you wish? Huh?"

The man in his grasp trembled. He begged for release but his pleas only encouraged Remus.

"You can't take us all at the same time."

Remus threw the miner to the ground. He pushed his way through the crowd, searching for the man with the quick-witted mouth. "Say something now. Say it. You coward. Hiding in the shadows like a frail kitten. Come forward if you are so brave."

The mob stepped back, allowing Remus to wend in between shoulders. He strode back to his stool and climbed up. The miners silent as they waited for his next statement. Remus could taste the danger in the air. His life depended on the next words that came from his lips. One wrong word and the mob would tear him to shreds and feed his flesh to the flames. He pointed his spear into the dirty faces that stared at him.

"I'll double the pay of each man who stays on to see this through. And we'll send a party to bring back fish and venison for our empty bellies." Remus watched the expressions shift away from hostility as the men calculated their potential earnings. "And I will forfeit my command to any man who believes he can best me in a battle to the death."

Miners glanced left and right, expecting nobody to accept the challenge from their feared boss.

Skunk slowly pushed his way forward from the back of the crowd. The mob gasped as they parted, giving wide berth to the behemoth who approached the fire.

Chapter Forty

Carson hid behind the furthest tent in the camp. He had difficulties spying on the miners from the forest. He wasn't tall enough to see past some of the tree limbs and James had already taken the prime spot across from the fire pit in the middle. Carson wished the wild man had stayed with him. Sitting up high on the creature's shoulders would have given Carson a spectacular view of the action.

He heard the swell of anger as men filed out of the mine and collected in the center of the camp. Carson rounded the right side of the tent and crept closer to the front. His view was obstructed by the supply wagon and stacks of crates. The solid wall closed him off from the swelling shouts and miners grouped together. Carson fell back and circled the left side of the tent. The new angle helped a tad. The supply wagon still eclipsed most of the gathering but at least he could now see the fire and the left side of the mob.

As the men screamed and carried on, Carson stared at Remus Phillips standing out front. He tried to calm the men but the noise reminded Carson of the big fights in the saloon back in Pella. When things got out of hand, men gathered and cussed and the calm slipped away to reveal the scary side of men. Carson had been so intent on following the scene that he hadn't noticed Dusty tromping across the camp. Carson jumped off the ground and scrambled to hide behind the tent. He ran without watching his steps and his right boot caught the support rope along the side of the tent. The peg shot out of the soil and slapped him in the back as he lunged headlong into the grass. The tent began collapsing into the middle as the one side had caved without its required support.

Carson crawled on his hands and knees, leaving his hat behind. He made it to the forest and tucked himself behind a stout trunk with a sprawling set of roots. The sound of Dusty's feet, shuffling along the dirt froze Carson's blood. He held his breath and waited for a few moments. Carson expected Dusty to pop out on his side of the tree and drag him back to Remus. After the longest couple of minutes in his life, Carson glanced around the base of the tree. He saw his hat, upside down next to the tent with the slack guide rope swaying above.

He glanced along the other side of the tree and found no sign of Dusty. Relieved, Carson used the raucous crowd noise to hide his trek to retrieve his hat. Carson stepped gently on the tips of his boots as if he feared wood boards to creak beneath his weight. He bent to grab his hat and brushed the dirt off the crown against his thigh.

With the speed of a lightning bolt, two arms stretched under the side of the tent, gripped Carson's ankles and tugged him down and inside the tent. The canvas whipped across his nose and stung his skin as he found himself in the half-collapsed tent staring up into Dusty's face.

"Well, looky here. I believe I caught the mouse that ate all our cheese." Dusty giggled as he palmed Carson's neck and pulled him to his feet. Dusty flung the tent flap wide and pulled Carson along towards the fire. Carson's boots dug ruts in the earth as he refused to move his feet. He clawed his jagged fingernails into Dusty's thick wrists but the muscle was so thick that the fingernails failed to raise a scratch in the man's flesh.

When they rounded the supply wagon, Dusty made a bold entrance, dropping Carson at Remus' feet by the fire. Carson blinked away the bright light as he looked about. Skunk stood in front of Remus and the miners had formed a semi-circle around them. Remus' grin stretched so wide it forced his eyes to shrink under the bushy brows. Skunk turned aside.

"Maybe this is where the food went." Dusty kicked sand in Carson's face. The grit burned his eyes and his teeth crunched it while he brushed away as much as he could.

Remus knelt before Carson. He lifted his chin with the smooth part of the spear. Carson kept his eyes closed because of the burning sensation. But he heard Remus' pleasure as he paid attention to the man's breathing.

"I told you all I would figure this out, didn't I?"

Nobody spoke. Remus grabbed Carson's hair and pulled him to standing. Carson squealed as the hair follicles strained to remain embedded in his scalp. He started to cry immediately, in pain and afraid. The hot tears increased his anguish as the sand rode the current behind his eyeballs.

"In some countries, tender flesh of children is a delicacy." Remus moved Carson closer to the flames. The yellow-orange heat flickered and danced like it attempted to taste the boy. "Too bad your brother died before he could witness your death. I'm sure he would have been relieved to unburden himself from a slow-minded albatross. Hm?"

Carson swung his fists at Remus. He remembered James' reaction whenever someone had cruelly referenced his disability. Even with the pain of his hair and eyes, Carson tried his hardest to land each strike on Remus' chin.

Remus laughed. The mob erupted into laughter as well. Remus stabbed Carson in the side of his neck with the spear. The sharp point broke the skin and hot blood flooded his shirt collar. Carson screamed, clutching at his wound. Remus allowed Carson to falter, flopping on the earth.

"I think everyone should take a turn teaching this bratty child a lesson for stealing our food. Perhaps he will apologize for making such a huge mistake." Remus glared at the miners as they cheered and howled. "IF - he survives to voice his apology."

The mob erupted into chaos. Shouts for revenge and making the boy pay rained down like a torrential maelstrom. Carson blubbered into the dirt as his hand clamped the stab wound from opening wide. He tasted blood on the back of his tongue. Carson shouted in his head for the wild man to save him.

And he prayed silently for James to come to his aid. Carson was terrified and alone.

Chapter Forty-one

Lok had dug a plot for the food supplies. He had squared off a section deep within the brush, about four feet by four feet and as deep as it was wide. They had lined the bottom and sides with a thick layer of pine needles to mask the scent from critters and protect the supplies from too much dirt. Once the stash was filled, they covered the top with a thicker layer of pine needles. Then the dirt was scraped over the hole and covered with fern plants that had been scrounged from random spots within reach. James placed large stones on each corner of the plot in case the top blended too well. He wanted to be sure the supplies could easily be recovered.

As the men toiled with the hole, the camp erupted in a fury. James smiled as he worked, mopping sweat from his forehead, and enjoying the sounds of trouble. The plan had worked as he had hoped. Hungry men made desperate men.

Once they secured the food, James and Lok would split up. Lok would remain hidden near the cache to scare off any animals that nosed around, looking for free snacks. James intended to collapse the entrance to the mine. Skunk had handed him a stick of dynamite. With the mine closed off and no rations to feed the miners, the operation would shut down and the revolution would escalate.

Lok patted the last of the ferns in place. His straw hat had fallen behind his head with the strap tugging at his throat. He brushed his hands together and sighed.

"Lok work hard. Lok hungry."

James smiled. "Great job, Lok. I'm hungry, too." He dug his fist into his back pocket and pulled two strands of jerky out. James handed one to Lok who nodded happily as he chewed fast.

"Slow down. You'll get a bellyache."

Lok ignored James and devoured the meat stick before James could eat half his own. Lok stared at the jerky as his tongue swabbed his lips and teeth. James snickered and handed the Lok the rest of his jerky. Lok shoved it into his mouth. James watched as Lok's right cheek bulged. He folded his arms, interested to see Lok's jaw work the stiff meat from side to side, grinding in his molars. James slapped Lok's shoulder and chuckled.

James noticed the tenor of the mob had changed since he had last paid attention. The general hostility had transformed into shouts with responses. James imagined a politician barking his platform from a raised boardwalk while the supporters below cheered after each proclamation.

Lok and James gazed around the side of the redwood. Remus stood above the miners, undulating and carrying on. James bristled as he clamored for control. From the back corner of the fire pit, a shadow filled the dancing flames and a silence draped over the congregation like a blanket soaked in rainwater.

His saliva dried up as James saw Carson. Dusty had dragged his best friend into the center of the show. Remus took advantage of the gift. He used Carson as a fulcrum to force his way back into command of the angry mob.

James jumped forward, ready to rescue Carson from danger until Lok yanked him back. The small man's power surprised James. His grip crushed James' shoulder, making him squirm with his body tilted down to break free. But it was no use.

"James no go. James dead. Lok go."

He whirled on the Chinaman. "No. He's my brother. I have to save him."

CHAPTER 41

The men struggled, each moment ratcheting into more violence. Lok held on tight as James shoved and kicked to get away. James tripped, slamming face first into the ground. His temper flared, adrenaline rushing through his veins. James punched Lok in the side of the head. Lok groaned, turned his head the other way and clamped tighter. James threw another punch but missed as Lok wriggled around his legs. As James raised his fist for another strike, a gigantic paw snatched his wrist and pulled him backwards.

James stared at the upside-down grimace of Skunk.

"James." Skunk barked at him from above. Lok released his legs and James climbed to his feet. He tried to brush past Skunk to get Carson but the giant man blocked his path. "You can't screw this up. Stick to the plan."

"And get Carson killed? That wasn't the plan." James shouldered into Skunk who threw him away easily. James pointed his finger, his face hot with rage. "Outta my way, Skunk."

Skunk closed the gap. He grabbed James by the throat and breathed stifling air in his face. "We stick to the plan and we get what we want. All of us." Skunk lowered James. His grip firm as he held James in place. "I will take care of Carson for you. Remus won't want to deal with me. If you run in there then everything else fails."

James' feet skittered in place. His legs ignored Skunk's request as they wished to carry him forward. He nodded, half agreeing with Skunk and half thinking of tricking Skunk so he could bolt past him.

"If anything happens to Carson, I will kill you." James shoved Skunk. The push didn't even displace the man from his position.

"If anything happens to Carson, I will let you."

James softened. He knew Skunk to be a man of his word and if he offered his head on a plate then who was James to question his intentions? A growing pit in his belly still fluttered with nervous energy.

Skunk snuck away to get back to the fire pit. James composed himself before heading for the mine. He said goodbye to Lok who faded into the shadows behind the food cache. James hurried between trees as he rounded the camp. He paused to check on the situation in the center. Remus stood upon his stool, rousing the miners into a lather, and swinging his spear in the air. James cracked his knuckles and rushed along his path to bring the operation to a halt.

Each moment felt like an eternity as his mind fretted over his little friend.

Chapter Forty-two

He gloated over his triumph. Remus had won the men over after a precipitous fall from his lofty throne. Dusty's delivery of the boy had saved his neck and not a moment too soon. Remus had felt the cloying peril suffocating him before Carson landed at his feet.

Remus had intelligence to understand his stay of execution would be temporary if he didn't solve the hunger crisis imminently. However, he would utilize the short reprieve as a release valve, harming the boy as he figured out next steps. His mind worked on a backup plan before anything else as an intrinsic survival response.

His boot pressed down on Carson's upper back. The boy squirmed and whined with his face in the dirt. The fire crackled, sending a pair of embers floating down onto Carson's exposed lower back. He clasped unsuccessfully at his flesh. Remus primed the fury. He directed two miners at the front of the crowd to come forward and take their turn with the boy. The first man, a rotund body filled to overflowing beyond the stretch of his suspenders, spat into his palms, rubbed them together with a gritty sound and slapped the boy's face hard. His filthy hands grabbed at Carson's head so both sides of his face could accept the punishment.

The men howled with delight. Cries for harsher means echoed from the middle of the humanity.

The second miner summoned forth elbowed the first man aside. He shined the tip of his boot with Carson's shirt. After admiring the glow of renewed leather, the man danced a two-step while humming aloud. He did a pirouette and then slammed the shined toe into Carson's ribcage. The boy shrieked; his cries muffled by the roar of pleasure. The second man held up his index finger to signal he had something to add. The mob hushed as dirty faces leaned forward for the next act. The miner shimmied his rear at the men in a lewd imitation of a dancing doxie, distracting the men while he unbuttoned his fly. The miner let loose with a generous stream of urine, both hands planted firmly on his hips, while the ammonia-smelling liquid drenched Carson's shirt and dungarees.

The crowd lost it. Laughter and slapped backs rolled through the crowd like a wave of wheat in a breezy pasture. Hats were tossed high into the air and a few men locked arms as they do-si-do'ed in small circles.

Remus pulled Carson up by the roots of his hair. Carson screamed. His face smeared with tears and snot; the dirt cleared away by the free-flowing currents. Remus sat Carson on his stool with a heavy shove. He steadied the boy from teetering over the back side. Remus moved behind Carson, his right hand on the boy's shoulder and the left hand directing the tip of the spear into the outer edge of his ear.

"Sit still, you blubbering baby."

He jabbed the spear into Carson's ear, far enough to create a sharp burrowing sensation inside his skull, but not hard enough to brain the boy. At least, not until he had a little more fun.

The mob egged on Remus. Calls for running the spear through and turning the boy on a spit over the fire reverberated into his face. Remus delighted in the surge of energy. He would put the men back to work while they filled their systems with hatred. His desire to destroy Carson and whoever else got in the way brimmed to his mind. He felt dizzy and his breath became erratic with the anticipation of the kill.

Remus twisted the spear a quarter turn. The end sunk deeper inside the boy's ear canal. Carson shrieked and strained against Remus' grasp.

CHAPTER 42

As he turned his wrist to drive the spear deeper, Skunk pushed his way to the front. The hulking man glared at Remus through insistent eyes. He bent slightly at the waist to whisper to Remus.

"James has returned."

Remus almost dropped the spear. His hands went numb and his fingers felt icy cold. Remus choked for air, realizing he had stopped breathing with the revelation. He searched Skunk's expression, challenging for lies. Skunk nodded and pointed towards his tent.

"I think James took the food." Skunk cleared his throat before whispering some more. "I hid his gun and knife. But they are gone."

Remus ignored the miners as they demanded more blood. He glossed over their dirty faces, confused about James. They had confirmed his death. How could he have come back from the dead? His brow furrowed as his memory worked through the moments in the forest. He had not seen James' body with his own eyes. Skunk and McCourty had verified his demise. Could they have been mistaken? Or had they pretended James was dead, knowing the truth would come around to haunt him to the end of days?

"You," Remus stammered. "You told me he was gone."

Skunk shrugged. "He wasn't breathing when we left him. We looked him over."

Remus pulled the spear away from the boy's head. A fresh flow of gore exited the stretched hole. He clutched Skunk's arm, caught between running off and demolishing every living being within reach.

"What do you want me to do, sir?"

Remus stared at Skunk's lips as the question unfurled but he hadn't comprehended the request. His brain walked several paths of decisions he needed to make. His urges for vengeance overtook his body's instinct for survival. Remus imagined how he could leverage Carson to draw James out. And if James failed to come forward, then Remus would know that

Skunk had hoodwinked him. Either way, Remus would satisfy his blood lust with death by his hand.

"Fetch him to me."

Skunk said he would do his best to find James but he had no idea where he had hidden. Remus nodded and pushed Skunk into the crowd. James would come out without a prolonged search because Remus had what James loved more than anything. His little brother. James would come fast once he saw what Remus was capable of, he told himself.

Remus laughed louder than the din at the fire.

Chapter Forty-three

The pain hurt worse than anything he had felt before. Carson choked on blood and snot. His head swam with dizziness, making the chaotic scene around the fire pit more monstrous. Faces contorted and stretched to absurd proportions. The shouts of the miners sounded muffled, like the voices came from inside a long tube. And that was only in his good ear. Carson heard nothing through his left ear but the sloshing of blood and the thumping of his punctured ear drum.

Carson clawed at the dirt. He tried to get away but Remus' heavy foot pinned him in place. He grasped at reality through the haze of wickedness that clouded his mind. Carson tried to remember when the wild men would come. They would flip the camp upside down and save him and James.

James.

Where was James? Carson cried harder when he realized James hadn't come to his rescue yet. He knew James was nearby. And Lok too. But nobody saved him from Remus' torture.

The fire's heat baked his legs. Carson used swimming motions in the sand to draw himself away from the flames. Remus allowed him to wiggle away just far enough to save his flesh. His lips puffed clouds of grit. Skunk pulled Remus aside, whispering something. The distraction provided Carson with a window of hope. He inched slowly from the boss man's circle of influence. His heart pounded harder as he thought he would finally escape the torture. A miner with a sunken chin and crossed eyes pointed out Carson was getting away. A few more men close by parroted the miner's observation.

Skunk left the circle in a hurry. Remus returned his attention to Carson, cutting his hopes of freedom like a bayonet striking to the bone of a soldier. The heel of Remus' boot dug into Carson's spine. The sharp pain lanced from his core to his extremities with the speed of lightning. Carson screamed. He flailed and fought against the punishment.

Remus yanked Carson to his feet with a fistful of hair. He dumped Carson onto the stool and steadied his trembling body with a stern hand upon his shoulder. Carson started to flinch away but Remus dug his fingernails into Caron's skin like the talons of a hawk.

"I ain't done with you yet, boy."

Carson stared at the morphing faces of men before him. The sea of onlookers swelled and crashed all around him. He watched their mouths stretch wide with hatred and evil intentions but their voices never reached his ears, instead sounding like dampened echoes deep inside the mine.

Remus showed his spear once more. The sharpened rod danced in front of Carson's face to the men's delight. Remus shoved one end into the ground in front of his stool. Then the man pushed Carson's face downward, dangerously close to the other sharp side. Carson's chin rested on the point, a new sharp pain stabbing through his jaw. Remus leaned harder and harder until the point of the spear drove into the flesh beneath Carson's chin. He erupted into a blood-curdling shriek. It felt hot and the pressure of the spear almost made it through the underside of his tongue. Blood filled Carson's mouth. He gagged and gurgled, choking on his own fluids.

"Come out now, James. Before it is too late." Remus bellowed. The miners glanced about in every direction, hoping to catch the first sight of the man who had been "killed" and now had come back from the dead. "Each second I wait for you is another minute off your brother's life."

CHAPTER 43

Carson faded in and out of consciousness. The hurt he experienced had been more than all his injuries in the past, added one upon the other. His mind rolled through moments with Mobay and James and Sarah. Carson smiled through the blood as he saw himself beating James at poker time and again. He coughed up a crimson clot that landed on the chinless miner's shirt. His eyes rolled back, following the memories of his days running through fields and hunting rabbits with James.

He saw his mother smiling at him, her tender fingertips stroking his cheek. She calmed him with her consoling kisses.

Remus pushed harder. The spear gouged the underside of Carson's tongue. He gave up the fight, his neck muscles relaxing, going with the flow instead of straining against Remus' strength.

The hand lifted from his scalp. Carson teetered on the stool. The only thing holding him up was the spear jammed into the bottom of his face.

Through the darkness, Carson heard James. His voice sounded angry. Distant. The crowd fell silent. Remus breathed heavily like he had run up a steep hill. He begged James to come save his brother. Carson tried to smile but his skin pulled tight from the impaling. James had really been more of a brother than a friend all these years. Carson knew the ruse was to have everyone believe they were brothers. But Carson had always felt it more reality than fiction. James and Carson.

Carson and James.

A battle ensued. More chaos in his personal space.

Carson screamed out to the wild man, a silent plea from deep within his brain. He begged the wild man to forget the plan. He needed his friend to come to his aid now. Carson waited for the voice, deep and guttural in his mind to respond. Only silence and his own desperation answered. Carson tipped over, falling to the earth in an excruciatingly slow process. The spear still lodged in his chin. He crashed to the ground, thankful for the release in pressure on his jaw. Where the pressure dissipated, the pain continued.

He felt the warmth of the fire on his skin. Carson wished the fire died out so he could cool off with the night air, drying the sweat from his brow and the staunching the flow of blood from his wounds.

For a moment, Carson's eyes recognized the starry heavens high above the clearing. He wanted to reach up and touch the sky, to see if it was real. As sparks of embers popped in his field of view, Carson thought they were shooting stars and he felt peace wash over his soul.

Chapter Forty-four

James rushed into the camp. He tossed Skunk aside like a paper doll, avoiding the large man's grasp. Time had run out on their plan and he could not afford to waste another moment conspiring with Skunk.

"Remus."

He shouted above the noise. Instantly, the mob of miners stopped cheering on their evil leader.

"Remus." James shouted once again.

The boss' throat bobbed. Remus stared at James with jaw agape and eyes wide. The reflection of dancing flames in his orbs reminded James of a ghostly encounter from his past.

"It's true. You are alive."

James hurdled the fire, landing behind the stool. Remus jumped backwards. At his feet, Carson lay in a pool of his own blood. James couldn't tell if Carson was alive or dead.

Remus pulled the spear from Carson's face. He shoved the dripping point in James' direction. "You never should have come back, James."

James pulled his knife. He fended the shiny blade against the spear. The miners back away and then fanned out to form a generous circle around the combatants. James could hear the raspy breaths and whispered bets between the men.

"I couldn't let you get away with murder." James crossed his right boot over his left, shifting his stance and forcing Remus to counteract. "Your abuse ends tonight."

Remus laughed. He jabbed the spear at James twice. Then Remus twirled the weapon between his fingers and held it at his side like a canoe paddle.

"You can't win, James." Remus nodded at the miners. "It's many against one."

James lunged forward. His blade aimed at Remus' throat but batted aside by the shaft of the spear.

"Are you sure the men are with you?" James feinted another strike before darting back, testing Remus and his reactions. Remus stepped back and then to the left. "You sound confident considering how you've treated them."

Remus glared at the men on the outer edge. "Without me, they can't survive. I feed them and pay them."

James laughed this time. "The food is gone. And by my calculations, you have yet to provide anyone with coins." James turned his attention to the crowd. "How many of you are tired and hungry?"

The miners' eyes checked with Remus before responding. Remus stepped toward the men. "We're all hungry and tired, James." He hocked up bile and spit at James' feet. "But YOU took the food. And YOU have caused all our delays. I think the men have YOU to thank for their condition."

James kicked sand up. A spray of grains flew into Remus' face. He gasped and blindly stabbed his spear forward, protecting against the sneak attack James had intended. James had ducked just in time, hearing the spear point whip past his head.

The enemies circled, testing each other with sudden dips and jabs. Both men sizing the other up. James began to question his urgency as he respected the deftness of his opponent. Remus was like a coiled rattlesnake,

CHAPTER 44

hissing and prepared to strike. He wondered if he had underestimated his foe, allowing his emotions and self-confidence to put him in harm's way.

Too late now, James. He coaxed himself on.

Remus charged James. The point of the spear aimed for his belly, James rolled to the right at the last second and swung his knife in a sweeping motion. The blade connected with Remus, scoring a gash along the man's forearm. His shirt flapped open, revealing a serious cut which bled freely. Without a grimace, Remus spun and charged again. James, leaning back on his rear foot, instinctively kicked his front foot, catching Remus in the gut. The shaft of the spear rolled up, rubbing the bridge of his nose. The pain forced hot tears to flood his vision.

James wheeled backwards and to the left. Remus landed with his weight leaning over the spear across his knees. He gasped for air with his deadly eyes never straying from James. The boss recovered quickly, twirling the spear in his fingers. James looked around for Lok or Skunk. He hoped someone would jump in and help him defeat Remus. The man had been dangerous with a switch and he provided just as much challenge with the homemade spear.

Remus dipped the spear's tip into the fire. He held it there for several seconds until the flames licked up the carved wood like a torch. Remus jabbed the fiery spear at James from multiple angles and with the speed of a mountain lion. James rolled, ducked, and side-stepped the onslaught. Each attack getting closer to connecting, so much so that James felt the heat of the flames on his flesh.

James swatted away the final attack with the blade of his knife. The force of the strike had been strong enough to knock his weapon free. The knife flew into the mob, men moving away so the blade fell to the ground behind them. The crowd closed into a tight circle without hesitation. James clenched his hands. He had nothing to defend himself with except his bare hands now.

Remus grinned. He stretched his back and gathered his wind. "Tough break, kid. But I told you there was no chance you could win. You should have paid attention to me."

The words stung James. Carson's wisdom echoed in his head from every game of cards they had ever played. James held his hands up to protect against another charge. He hazarded a glance at Carson who remained in a heap along the fire's edge. James steeled himself for the battle of his life. He knew the fight between he and Remus had become much more - it was a fight for survival. For he and Carson.

James stepped to his left, circling closer to Carson. He called his friend's name, attempting to get a reaction. The boy didn't move a muscle. James called him again.

Before he could gauge Carson's condition, Remus came at James with renewed vigor. The man screamed like a crazed Indian on a warpath. The sound startled James more than the fiery spear tip which shot for his face. James blinked and swung his arms to deflect the oncoming strike.

Chapter Forty-five

He had James right where he wanted him. Locked in a fight to the death, with all his men gathered around for support. And if the miners failed to stick up for Remus, then he would have their heads on pikes. Skunk and Dusty would line them up for Remus to run them through with his spear.

James threw his hands up to fend off the maneuver but he had been a fraction too slow. The spear's flaming point skidded across his neck, cutting through flesh, and burning the wound shut simultaneously. Blood flowed from the rear portion of James' neck. He clutched at his injury, choking through his bloodied fingers.

Remus hurried into striking position again. The flame had snuffed out when the spear dug through his enemy's throat. Remus shrugged off the lack of fire and stabbed at James a second time. The tip gouged through the center of James' outstretched palm. He had only a fraction of a second to defend himself and his instincts to ward off the shot sacrificed his right hand. James dropped to his knees, staring in horror at the hole in his fist. Remus closed his left eye to stare at James through the circular opening.

He cackled with delight.

James scrambled to his feet, his left hand grasping his neck and the right hand dangling at his side, dripping blood onto the ground. His teeth gnashed at the pain. Remus wanted to finish him off whole he had the upper hand. He swung the spear like a club, glancing a blow off his foe's forearm. James took the abuse, refusing to remove the hand from his throat. He kicked a screen of sand at Remus. The bold attack caught Remus unawares, too consumed with his impending victory.

Remus cursed and swatted grit from his face with the bloody sleeve. The crimson swirled the dirt around his face, casting an ominous pagan reflection over the flames. The miners gasped. Remus crunched particles between his molars. He spit the excess and charged James. As he ran the tip at his head, James lowered his shoulder, absorbing Remus' momentum in a thunderous collision of bones and meat. The spear flew forward. Both men collapsed into a pile. James scored the higher ground due to his position. Remus threw his forearm upward, connecting with James' nose. The cartilage cracked and blood squirted down into Remus' mouth. He bucked to throw James off. While James attempted to climb up from all fours, Remus rolled up and dove onto his back. Remus wrapped his arms around James' head, pulling back so his grip could suffocate James. His arms missed the sweet spot, buried beneath James' chin - instead locked across his chin.

James roared and shifted his jaw lower. His teeth sunk into Remus' arm, the same arm that his knife had slashed earlier. Remus shrieked and loosened his grip to escape the bite but James had a lock on the flesh. His teeth tore and shredded skin and sinew. Remus ripped his arm away, agonizing over the rapid burn of mangled muscle. James turned over, gagging, and spitting hunks of what used to be connected to Remus' arm.

Remus growled. He stomped to his lost spear on the other side of the fire. His good hand dragged along the underbrush feeling around for the stick. His fingers glanced across something wooden. He lifted the stick but found only dead wood sloughed off by a local pine. Remus felt around until he discovered the spear within four feet of the mistaken branch. He rounded to find James hunched forward, still sick from the gore in his mouth.

Raising the spear over his head, Remus sunk the weapon into James' exposed back. He aimed for the center of his spine, hoping to incapacitate

CHAPTER 45

James to the point the boy could do nothing to hamper Remus' horrific example. The point struck the ground, fully lodged through James' back and jutting from his chest. James screamed in a breathless whisper. His body slid down the spear, tracking blood behind him and slurping as his flesh allowed the rest of the spear to get swallowed up in bodily juices.

Remus yanked on the spear, trying to free the wood from his enemy. He knew the exit would double up the damage. But the body clung to the knotted wood. Remus tugged and pulled, unable to clear the spear. He decided to rotate the shaft like a maid churning butter, tearing the hole wider in each direction as he put his weight behind it. The spear broke free with splashing sound like a rock skipped into a river.

The miners stood motionless; breath held tight as they took in the terrifying scene. Slowly, pockets of men hooted and clapped for their boss. They hung on the air, hoping to catch the death blow in all its glory and bloodshed. Hands held out for winnings as the ones who bet on Remus wished to collect their winnings.

Remus, exhausted and bloodied, raised his gory spear to the moon. He howled like a wolf, calling his pack to the kill for leftovers. The vocalization thundered over the shouts of the mob. Remus felt like a warrior, baring his teeth at the audience, challenging and defying the world to fall at his feet in worship or death. He shoved his way into the crowd, leaving his bloody mark upon each chest and arm pushed aside. Remus knelt inside a newly formed circle of men. His fingers closed around James' knife. The blade felt heavier than he had anticipated in his fist. Remus rose and strode to the prone foe who did little but beg for breath and bleeding out across the camp.

He stood above James, huffing and brushing blood away from his brow with his sleeve. Remus crouched. He tugged James' head backwards with a fistful of filthy hair, exposing the boy's neck. Remus lowered the blade until it rested under James' left ear, poised an inch or two higher than the semi-cauterized wound from the spear.

He pushed the sharp edge of the blade into the tender flesh. The miners coaxed him, implored him to finish what he had started. Remus saddened because he would need to find a new foil now to exercise his anger on. He thought James would have been more of a worthy opponent considering the bravery. But in the end, James would die like any other weaker man.

Remus nodded at the mob. He screamed at the heavens and tightened his grip on the knife.

Chapter Forty-six

The encampment erupted with fury. Carson lay still. His body wracked with pain, he chose to play possum while Remus had been distracted. It took all his might to remain still when Remus pulled the spear free of his chin. It had felt like hot fire searing his skin. He tasted blood and it made his stomach churn with nausea. Carson left his mouth open so the blood would drain into the dirt instead of collecting in the back of his throat.

He listened to the approach of James. His best friend answering the call, coming to his aid. Carson wasn't naive anymore. He knew James stepped forward more out of his anger to fight Remus, not to defend his buddy. Regardless, Carson took comfort for the break in his torturous treatment.

The clash resounded above him and to the right. Carson felt the mob shift closer to the fire. A few boots kicked into his chest as the men stepped over him to get a better seat at the battle. He used the cover to inch his way across the ground. Each movement aroused blinding agony as his body fought to clot his gaping holes. His left ear remained closed off to noise. Carson awaited another mass migration so he could make some larger gains in his escape.

A miner stepped on his legs, forcing Carson to bolt up to his right elbow. The boot placement felt so deliberate and full of weight that Carson could not believe it had been accidental. As the miner glared down at him, Carson folded into the earth, blinking his eyes to pretend he had faded out.

The man must have been satisfied with his play-acting because the mine grunted and chuckled before moving forward. Carson rubbed the bruised flesh through his dungarees, careful to do so with scarcely moving fingers.

WE ARE HERE.

Carson froze. He heard the voice in his skull even though it sounded tinny and like it only penetrated one side of his mind.

WHERE ARE YOU, LITTLE ONE?

Clawing through the soil, Carson finally reached the back side of the mob. He crawled as quietly as he could, afraid to give away his plan. The din of the battle overshadowed his movements but he still tried to creep delicately. He answered the wild man, asking him for help. Carson tried to describe his location but his words failed, his brain muddled from the shock and injuries. Carson repeated several times, he was behind the miners and moving towards the forest. But with trees all around the camp, his location wasn't particularly accurate.

A massive paw gripped the back of his shirt and lifted him into the air. Carson's eyes bounced in their sockets as the world quaked all around him. Stepping into the shadows of the tree line, Carson was placed down, his back against a redwood.

Skunk hovered over his upturned face.

"Stay here, Carson." Skunk glanced over his shoulder at the fight.

Carson sagged, allowing his body to fold into itself. Every fiber of his being screamed for nursing. The blood in his mouth had grown thicker as it absorbed his saliva, forming a coppery paste on his tongue.

"I'll take care of the mine. And I'll make sure James comes to you. Just stay put."

Skunk itched his wild mane before disappearing along the tree line. Carson's eyes only followed him a few paces until it would have forced him to turn his head and strain his wounded neck.

The earth trembled under his rear. Distant and small but growing heavier and closer. The wild man assured Carson they were here to restore

CHAPTER 46

order. He asked Carson to remain in place so he wouldn't get caught up in the destruction. Whoops and shrieks tore through the forest, vibrating anything that wasn't rooted into the soil. Carson's chest shook. He clenched his eyes shut against the mayhem.

The woods blew up in a fray of chaos. Limbs snapped louder than gunshots. Whole trees teetered and crashed to the ground as if a massive storm consumed the woods. Men screamed and ran for their lives. Carson twitched as he heard bones break and skulls cave in. He knew it was dying men because their screams cut out immediately rather than trailing off.

He prayed for James. And for his wild men family. Carson had never seen a war, nor been close enough to the action before. His heart hammered with fright as the world exploded in every direction. Carson begged the wild man to find James and bring him to his side. The voice didn't answer his request. He was left with his own shaky internal voice, praying for safety, and hanging on to live to the next day.

Mobay hunched next to Carson. He wrapped his long, hairy arm around Carson's shoulders. Carson lost his control, falling into his friend's embrace. He cried and screamed, drowned out by the sparse hair and chiseled muscles on Mobay's chest. His friend told him to keep his mind clear so his father wouldn't discover his disobedience. The wild man had insisted Mobay and his mother stay in their nest, safe and far from trouble. But Mobay could not pass up a chance to help his new human friend. And he wanted to follow in his daddy's footsteps, bringing the fight to evil men.

Carson nodded into Mobay's body. He whispered through his tears.

"Like me and James."

He sunk deeper into the safety of Mobay's presence, listening to the war that threatened to eliminate all trees and people from the northern part of California. Carson pulled himself free and crawled around the trunk to watch the battle.

Enormous shadows darted left and right. Fire had spread from the pit, lighting many of the ferns and grasses along the clearing. Some trees had fallen across the encampment like bridges from east to west. Lodged under one of the trees was a trail of bodies. Most flattened and splattered in blood. A few twitched or moved like they had a chance of crawling out from under the wreckage.

Carson shielded his face, sorry he had been too curious to mind his business.

Chapter Forty-seven

James hung on. Bloodied and pinned to his deathbed, James urged his spirit to continue the fight. His body failed to respond. Remus sat atop his back with the sharp blade pressed to his throat. The sensation remained vivid even if his body tumbled down a steep rabbit hole without the energy to fight his oppressor.

Remus flew headfirst, sprawling across the dirt. The miners sucked in a unified breath as the surprise sent their boss flying. Skunk's crotch slid across James' back and head as his momentum carried him over the top, merely a foot behind Remus.

His neck, weak and no longer supported by the tug of Remus' fist, collapsed forward, plunging James' face into the dirt. His brain commanded his neck to roll to the right so his breathing could improve. But his muscles surrendered to the exhaustion.

Skunk shoved his paws under James' arms, helping him to his knees. The piercing fire where the spear had driven through his shoulder hollered in a white blaze. His vision blinded, James waited for the next assault. Remus cursed Skunk for interrupting his moment of glory. Before Remus could swoop in, Skunk hefted James to his feet, encouraging him to fight back.

"Now the fight is fair, James. Get after it."

The words had been blotted out by the furor within the mob. Miners rushed forward to join the fray. Skunk kicked two men away as he held James up. Remus, inflamed by the disruption, began casting miners aside as he trudged back to James and Skunk. James flopped forward, his body continuing to disappoint him without Skunk's staunch support.

As Remus rushed at them, Skunk launched James like a steam engine barreling down on a herd of cattle. His body hurtled like a human projectile, collecting Remus and another man who had decided to get involved. All three men tumbled together, kicking up clouds of dust and knocking latecomers down.

James raised up on one elbow. The camp had devolved into a stampede. Men charged in every direction, boots stepping on the limbs of those who had lost balance. The shouting impaired his senses more than the dust because he couldn't see anything through the crowds. His head pounded as heavily as his heart. James started to crawl towards safety when someone gripped him around his waist.

Remus had climbed on his back. James felt the strong hands locking around his belly, squeezing him from escaping and gathering more oxygen. James threw his head backwards, hoping to connect with Remus' face. But Remus remained lower across his back. Using every ounce of power left in his system, James rolled over onto his back, acquiring the high ground on Remus. The boss man released his grip around James' stomach so he could rain punches into the sides of his head. James absorbed the first flurry of blows before wheeling his head back. This time, his skull caught Remus in the chin. The echo of teeth gnashing together zipped through his head. Remus screamed, clutching his jaw.

James glanced about. He had hoped to find his knife or something he could use to help defend himself but the melee hid the possibilities from view. He looked for Skunk, unsuccessful to locate his only backup in the brawl. James took a few kicks as miners joined the fight. He tried to make himself small by leaning down over Remus. Several boots caught Remus in the torso and legs, his howling spurred by each new strike. James cocked back his fist. His hand had little force behind it as his body tried to regroup. Wasting no time, James lowered his elbow into Remus' chest instead.

Gravity did what his extremities couldn't. He raised up and slammed his elbow down. The second blow crunched ribs or breastplate. The sickening sound didn't deter James from trying again. As he lifted his arm for another strike, Remus turned far enough that the elbow smashed into earth. The less forgiving surface reverberated until James felt his brain shimmy in its case.

From somewhere deep in the mob, Skunk implored James to finish the battle. James furrowed his brow, frustrated with his inability to crush Remus in his weakened state. Remus, injured but in better command of his faculties, threw his shoulder into James' ribs. The shock blasted the wind from his lungs. James refused to fold and forced his will to carry on. He rose on unsteady feet, facing off with Remus who had risen as well.

"Step back. Give us room." Remus harangued the men. His orders went unheeded until the miners pulled each other away to let the men fight one on one. Remus shook his jaw from side to side with his bloodied hand. His face scrunched, the pain evident in his expression. James noticed a few blank spaces along the man's lower teeth.

James faltered. His feet stumbled as he collected his strength. Blood flowed from his shoulder and hand, and his face leaked crimson too. His shoulders slumped forward. His body begged for mercy, straining to fold forward and rest upon his knees. But James refused to give Remus any satisfaction. If he were going to die by Remus' hands, James would do so like a warrior, fighting to the very end and never giving up until his heart stopped beating.

Remus charged when the miners tucked along the fringes. His broken jaw hung limp like a thousand-year-old mummy's skull. James braced for the attack, shifting his weight from his right foot to his left and sliding the left leg forward. He tucked his head and shoulder to absorb the collision. At the last second, something buried within the sinews of his legs shot his knee upward. It caught Remus in the groin and the boss dropped to his knees in the spot where he had received the shot. His jaw clapped together as a groan rumbled from his manly region.

James lost his balance. He fell on top of Remus. Both combatants writhed, arms and legs intermingled in a stack of fleshy kindling. James stared down into Remus' slack-jawed face. He grinned as Remus' eyes grew wide, sensing the danger which hovered above.

James swung his head forward. His forehead obliterated the nose and left cheek of his former boss.

Chapter Forty-eight

Things hadn't gone as he had expected. Remus had believed himself to be the superior man. And with the company behind him, there was supposed to be no downside to conquering James Johnson. If James got the upper hand, then his men would have his back. And if they failed to back him up, then Remus would see to a slow and deliberate death for those who bet on the wrong horse.

Now, he found himself on the brink of defeat. Remus used the tip of his tongue to feel around his mouth. Missing teeth and a lower jaw that no longer sat properly in its cradle left Remus shaken but far from deterred. Even with a broken nose and a fractured cheekbone, Remus liked his chances for defeating James. It would just require more viciousness to prevail.

Remus tasted the blood as it drooled from the slack cavity that should represent a mouth. He let the mixture of saliva and blood pour from his open jaw. Remus gently pressed on the cheek which had ballooned to a distorted knot of pressure beneath his eye. His fingers traced the bump to the spot where a proud family heirloom had once divided his face. The cartilage gave way, unable to support the ridge of his nose which had been pressed inward and to the right. Remus sniffled through the blockage and choked on the fluids which drained down his throat.

He glowered at James. His foe sat dazed, distant while he rubbed along his bloody forehead. Remus smiled, if it could still be considered a smile, happy to see James suffered as well from his head butt. Remus climbed to one knee.

The ground shook.

A swell of panic overtook the miners surrounding the last moments of the fight. Men screamed and ran for safety. Their organs rattled inside their chests as thunderous howls and grunts broke from the forest. Gigantic shadows darted through the camp, eclipsing the flames. Remus stared at the monsters that stepped forth from the redwoods, snapping boughs and shivering trees. Whoops and knocks echoed from the far reaches of the woods, providing a rhythmic backdrop to the destruction which unfolded all around him.

Remus gulped.

Skunk ran towards Remus with terror etched in his face. His eyes wide and searching for a place to hide from the wild men. Skunk's crazy hair bounced in the draft of his wake, barely hiding the contorted grimace of a wild man trailing close behind him. The large man scooped James into his arms and shoved past Remus.

Remus shouted after Skunk, pointing out his cowardice for running when he could be saving his boss from trouble. As Remus shifted his attention back to the way from which Skunk had come, he stared into the eyes of obsidian horror. The wild man tore Remus's arm from its socket. The limb came free with a nauseating crack. Blood geysered, coating man and beast alike within range. Remus shrieked from the depths of his diaphragm but not a sound passed his dangling jaw.

He flopped onto his rear.

Miners climbed over one another in hapless attempts to outrun the creatures, leaving their dead coworkers behind. One miner broke in half when his tossed body clashed with a redwood. The spine folded neatly in two and the flesh parted around the trunk. Another miner tripped on a root. He scrambled to run again until he was flattened to the ground, a

CHAPTER 48

giant hairy foot smooshing his frame into the soil. His innards explode in all direction as the pressure forced the insides out.

Remus choked on blood.

Two wild men pulled at opposite ends of an older miner. The man's skeleton cracked and snapped free as he was pulled like a chicken's wishbone. The monsters hurled their parts high into the treetops.

The wild man snatched Remus up. The crushing grip pulled Remus by his nape, lifting his body off the ground. The lofty height provided a bird's eye view of the mayhem that swallowed the encampment. Burning beyond the original space, the fire had spread towards the underbrush, flames catching brambles and grass. The pattern of light snaked through the nearby forest and wended towards tents which had been positioned near the center of the site.

Remus kicked his legs, hoping to free himself from the monster's clutches. One of his boots flew off as his motions grew more desperate. Remus croaked, screaming for help without a sound. He trembled as he watched miners ripped apart and hurled through the air. Cries for mercy were drowned out by the carnage the wild men brought to the human invaders. Several wild men ran up enormous redwoods, using their feet like hands and clasping dead or dying men in their arms as they rushed to the canopy.

Skunk jumped up, grabbing at Remus' ankles. After a few attempts, Skunk got a hold of Remus and used his body weight to tug the boss towards the ground. The wild man allowed the foreman to lower Remus. He stepped back into the shadows as Skunk hovered over Remus.

"This could have been avoided. You've destroyed us."

Remus laughed through the gaps in his teeth. His lips curled against the grain of his sagging mouth. Remus pointed up at Skunk's face with his remaining arm.

"Bring me the boy." He gagged on a collection of fluids in the back of his throat. "And James."

Skunk nodded and stepped aside. In the place where his foreman had just stood, James glared down at Remus. His stomach churned and his skin crawled with animosity. Remus wanted to extinguish James' life and he would do so with his dying breath.

Remus waved James closer. James approached, inches at a time, never once breaking the eye contact with Remus. The boss lumbered to his feet. He dove at James, no strength or speed in his movements. James easily sidestepped, even in his battered condition. Remus gathered himself to try again. He clawed his way on top of the bodies of several dead miners, leaning heavily against their meat so he could face off with James.

"Tonight is the end."

Chapter Forty-nine

James teetered on shaky legs. He could not remember the last time he had felt so drained of energy. The physical toll had dragged down his mental faculties and erased all emotional tendrils. The battle had left an empty shell of a man. A cicada husk stuck to a tree long after the insect had perished.

He limped forward. Remus leaned backwards over a pile of dead miners. His lids drooped as the life fled his frame through the gaping shoulder socket. James wished to rid the world of the evil man, but he knew a quick death would be too good for Remus.

He needed to suffer.

James shuffled closer and slammed his bloody fist into the gory wound. His knuckles scraped bone, a fragment of which poked free of the torso. Remus gritted his teeth, wincing through the agony but careful not to scream. James understood the man's pride would never allow him to give James the satisfaction.

The melee abruptly halted as the wild men circled in. A forest of hairy beasts surrounded the center of the camp, enclosing James and Remus James staggered backwards. He clutched at this sopping shoulder, afr to look down and see flame light through the hole.

A high-pitched wail cut through the night, a stark siren agai hushed aftermath. James glanced over his wound to find Carsor into the circle. His little friend held James' lost knife poised abc

Carson's face, covered in dried blood and filth, contorted in a rage like a soldier charging down a battlefield hill to gut his enemy.

The knife sunk deep. Only the handle stood outside Remus' heaving chest. Carson yanked at the knife, using all his might to pull the blade free but it had been snagged by bone and muscle. Remus stared down at the knife, his eyes wide with disbelief, refusing to admit that a small boy, one with the mind of a toddler, had killed him. Remus shifted his gaze to Carson, who cussed and beat the body with his fists since he could no longer jam a knife into the man.

James forgot all his injuries. He grabbed Carson around his waist and hauled him away from Remus. Carson twitched and shook inside his arms. James buried Carson's face in his chest, running his hands through Carson's hair to soothe his friend. Carson bellowed, continuing his war cry inside the fabric of James' shirt.

Remus spit up blood, darker and thicker than the fluids that gushed from his missing arm. He tried to speak but the gore and the disconnected jaw prevented him from anything intelligible.

The wild man crouched and spun Carson around. James flinched at the sudden separation. He nearly reacted with violence towards the wild man until he realized the creature had needed to speak with Carson. James wished he could understand the silent conversation that transpired between Carson and the wild man. A smaller beast moved into range and joined in the discussion. Both beings nodded and consoled Carson with caresses.

One rose to his full height. He lofted Remus into the air by his ⟨...⟩ss stared into the creature's eyes. The wild man roared. ⟨...⟩d James and Carson to hold their heads against ⟨...⟩ed within their chests and stomachs. All the ⟨...⟩ining in the deafening howl, bending trees, and ⟨...⟩of the fire.

CHAPTER 49

With a free hand, the wild man twisted Remus' body completely around. His neck cracked like a ship run aground during a storm, dashed upon a rocky shore. The fight in Remus snuffed out. His legs and arm dropped lifeless.

Dead eyes open, Remus stared south while his body faced north.

The wild man tossed Remus into the hot embers which glowed orange red in the darkness. His corpse caught fire and rekindled the flames that had recently blown out from the howls.

Carson hugged the smaller wild man as the creatures retreated peacefully into the dark forest. The giant wild man returned to embrace Carson before carrying the smaller beast on his shoulder. The pair disappeared into the redwoods quietly, not a sound of their travels above the crackle of the fire.

James dropped to his knees. He slumped into the ground and closed his eyes. Every pinpoint of pain arrived where he had last forgotten about them. His head pounding and the holes in his body vacillated between sharp and dull throbs. Carson flopped next to James. He curled into a ball and tucked himself into the crook of James' arm.

"Thanks for killing Remus. But I could've done it myself."

Carson sniffled. He rubbed his nose into James' clothes.

"I didn't killed him. But I wanted to."

James thought about the admission. He suddenly realized he would never have expected to hear Carson say something so harsh. His heart saddened that Carson had been pushed to a new edge in his life. A dark side that any boy should be spared of knowing.

"What did the wild man say to you?"

Carson lifted his face. He blinked away tears and rubbed his nose dry with his sleeve.

"He said he would killed Remus so I could stayed innocence."

James fought his own tears. His mind wrestled with the humanity a wild beast had understood when humans tore each other apart like savages. He had been wrong about the wild men, not trusting them and fearing their animalistic behavior. Instead, the wild creatures had proved to be superior in their relationship with all living beings.

"Carson," James said as he choked up. "Carson, I paid attention this time." He ruffled Carson's hair. "We have to tell everyone about the wild men so people will let them live in peace."

Carson squeezed James tight. His ribs screamed but James ignored the pain, happy to be reunited with his best friend. Happy Carson was safe once more. And happy to be finished with the Phillips Mining Company. But most of all, delighted to be finished with Remus Phillips.

"Let's set here awhile. Everything hurts and I don't want to move until next week."

Carson giggled and slumped his body into place next to James.

Chapter Fifty

Skunk shook their hands and smiled. A light breeze parted his salt and pepper mane in different directions. It amazed James to watch as the man's hair took on a variety of shapes. He wondered how a man could capture so much hair under a hat and then realized it was probably the reason Skunk went without one.

The miners who had survived the wild men toiled with their work. It had taken three days to piece the camp together and re-establish operations. Dusty and Skunk worked tirelessly to convince the men that they would be paid for their loyalty and service. Skunk had worked out a deal with the survivors, they would be allowed to keep as much gold as they could carry on their person provided they finished the work for the mining company. And with a promise to back up Skunk's rendition of the events that had occurred to date. Skunk intended to tell Mr. Phillips the truth about the expedition, minus the involvement of any man in the death of his son, Remus.

"What will you boys do next?" Skunk slapped a hefty paw on James' back. He had been careful to avoid the sling which held James' shoulder dressing in place. But the slap shook the stitches beneath the poultice, nonetheless.

"Probably head home to Texas."

Skunk nodded, squinting against a ray of sunshine which glared along his face.

"So Texas is where you call home. Funny, I never took you boys to be Texans."

James glanced at Carson. His friend kicked a rock with the tip of his boot. He chose to avoid filling in the blanks of their past and let Skunk believe they were native to the Lone Star state.

"You think they'll go along with the plan?" James pointed at the men along the sifters. His fingers tingled as the motion stretched the scabbed wound in the center of his palm.

Skunk laughed heartily.

"Sure will. They're smart enough to walk away with Mr. Phillips' wages plus a hefty pocket full of ore for themselves. Too rich of a deal for any man to pass up."

Dusty waved at the trio from the mine opening. He had wished James and Carson well earlier. The burly man had apologized for his part in their trouble. Dusty begged forgiveness as he had done what he thought would save his own skin at the time. James had accepted the man's apology but he still resented the cowardice of one who he had looked up to before. Carson had ignored the request for forgiveness. He walked away from Dusty without a word. James told Dusty Carson would come around someday but he didn't believe his own explanation.

And James would not blame Carson after how he had suffered at the campfire thanks to Dusty dragging him to Remus.

Skunk handed James a burlap sack full of gold flakes and chunks. The heaviness surprised James since the bag had only been half full. Skunk had offered to throw in a little extra since James and Carson would miss collecting their wages. Skunk planned to count them as part of the deceased when he explained the attack on the camp.

"I hope Mr. Phillips buys the story. He won't be happy to learn of his son's passing. Or the missed deadline." James chewed on his lower lip.

"Phillips is a businessman. He invests knowing full well some bets won't pay off." Skunk rubbed his hands together with a leathery scraping sound. "The mine has proved fruitful. It took longer. So what."

"And Remus?" James feared for Skunk when he revealed how Remus perished.

"Truth be told?" Skunk leaned closer as if he needed to whisper his thoughts, even when nobody stood a chance of overhearing him. "Romulus is the favorite. Mr. Phillips can't stand Remus."

James nodded, figuring how Remus had come to be the boss far from home. Mr. Phillips used Remus' strengths to his own advantage while serving the dual purpose of keeping his offspring away.

"I best get back to work." Skunk shook hands again. "Take care of yourselves. I ain't never met a pair of brothers like you before. Stubborn as mules and braver than pissed off snakes." Skunk laughed. He slapped James in the back, forcing James to lunge forward. Skunk retreated to the mine, turning for one last weave before disappearing into the dark opening.

James whistled. Carson came running back to his side.

"Time to get moving, huh?"

Carson shielded his eyes from the sun. He nodded and held onto James' hand like he used to do years ago as a younger boy. The gesture surprised James after so long but he reveled in the closeness it provided. His mind recalled all their adventures and how much his little friend meant to him. James didn't want to bring harm to Carson anymore. He strongly considered going back to Texas so they could lead a long, boring life on the farm with his mother and George.

"We have one more thing to take care of before we go."

Carson walked alongside James. They said goodbyes to miners as they passed them. Most of the men would not get the chance to wish them well since they were busy up to their elbows in digging for gold.

They found Lok as he exited the mine with shoulders weighed down with buckets of soil. He grinned, dropping the buckets at his feet. James handed Lok the sack of gold Skunk had given him. He told Lok to use the funds to get back to his family in China. James suggested Lok pay off his family debts and live as a free man in his home country, far from the usury of men in California.

Lok wept, shaky hands rubbing the sack between his palms. He thanked James and Carson for being his friends and reminding him that not all white men were bad. Lok promised to put the gold to effective use saving his family. He asked if James and Carson would visit him in China so he could introduce them to all his brothers and sisters and cousins. James lied and said they would be happy to meet them someday soon.

Lok hugged James tight. Carson squeezed in between them and the three held each other through tears and heavy hearts.

Chapter Fifty-one

James and Carson took their time hiking through the mountainous terrain. Their packs had been overstuffed with food supplies to last a week. James offered to carry Carson's pack while it weighed him down but Carson refused to give in. He wanted to prove he was as much a man as James. His neck ached from the strain across his shoulders. Carson braved it out, hoping James would allow them to take frequent breaks.

Carson smiled to himself. He listened to the voices in his head.

The days passed with plenty of sweat and exhaustion. Each night, James and Carson gave in to their soreness. They would set a small fire and gobble down some hard tack and coffee before falling fast asleep beneath the stars. James promised to hunt for some rabbit or deer meat but he collapsed at the end of the daily trek. Most times before Carson finished eating his supper.

He never got scared, awake alone at night in the wilderness. The voices kept him company. And Carson knew his friends would never permit a mountain lion or bear to harm him. Carson enjoyed the company even if he couldn't see them face to face.

James argued aloud that they would return to Texas to farm and set their roots in the soil. Hours later, he would pontificate another destination along the northwest. James mentioned places like Alaska, Montana, and Idaho. Carson laughed at the sound of each one. He wondered who chose the names for towns and states, and where the words came from. Carson figured wherever they ended up, the boys would look for work and start the process all over again.

Unless they went back to Texas.

Mobay had followed their travels with his father. His friend explained that his elders had given into the restlessness of his youth. They reasoned it would be easier to shepherd him through his maturation than confine him to the nest or the den. Mobay compared himself to Carson and his father to James. But Carson replied that James was not his daddy. The difference meant little to Mobay.

James had no idea Carson spoke with the wild men. The creatures kept pace quietly, out of range and hidden within the recesses of the trees and plants. Carson knew they were nearby and he decided to keep the secret in case James became angry with the wild men. When dusk swooped in, the wild men moved closer, using the shadows to mask their outlines. Carson would know where to find them based on the direction their voices came from inside his head. He couldn't make out their features but he would catch their form peeking around a trunk or find their glowing eyes blinking above the underbrush. He liked to search for them because it reminded Carson of the games he used to play with James a long time ago. Hide and seek. Sometimes, Carson wished they could go back in time and carry on like they used to. His mother would be there, too.

Eventually, the wild men told Carson they had to return to their clan. The goodbyes were short and distant, but just as painful for Carson. He knew his friends had to stay in the forests. However, Carson liked to imagine the family coming to live with them in Texas. Not only would he have a blast showing Mobay around the farm, but his chores would be simplified. The wild men were so big and strong that they could feed the animals, clean the pens, plant seeds, and harvest the growth faster than anyone. Carson wondered where they would be able to hide the wild men when James brought him back to reality.

"I've been thinking about what to do."

Carson rolled his eyes. He had heard the same beginning numerous times and it never ended with a final decision.

James hunkered down against a tree. He tilted his hat back as the shade cast a wide net around his resting spot.

"You can't go home. Not unless you can prove yourself to be far richer or more grown up."

Carson broke a twig into smaller pieces then cast the bits into the sunlight, one at a time.

"We gotted lots of gold now, James. Ain't we richered?"

James shook his head. "Naw. It's not enough to impress people. Probably only pay off the debts and buy a few new things."

Carson shrugged. He pictured himself playing with lots of toys in a big bedroom. The other children in town jealous as they came calling for him every day. And he imagined the shiniest, new deck of cards with poker chips made of ivory. Carson sat at a table in a saloon with crowds of onlookers while he used his wealth to gamble and beat card sharps from all around.

"I made up my mind. We're going to see the Rocky Mountains and find out what all those mountain men made noise about. Whaddaya say, Carson?"

James slapped his knee and started to fold his arms across his chest until the pain in his stitches made him think better of it. Carson shook his head. His best friend wanted to change, talked about becoming a man and living an adventurous life. But the more he tried to change, the more James stayed the same.

And Carson was fine with it. As long as he spent all his time with James, they could go anywhere in the world.

"Can we play cards now? My legs hurted." Carson rustled inside his sack for his dog-eared deck.

"Sure, buddy. I'm tuckered out myself."

Carson's tongue danced along the corners of his lips. His hands worked furiously to shuffle the deck and deal the cards. He hid his grin as the cards facing him revealed three of a kind. James grimaced at his hand, moving one card from the left to the right.

"Dangit." James huffed and threw the cards down.

Carson giggled and thought of razzing James about not paying attention. But he decided James had been through enough recently. Carson would take the wins quietly for now.

Show Your Support for Indie Authors

I hope you enjoyed this book and will read more stories from Chuck Buda.

Want to really help an indie author? Take a moment to leave a review on Amazon, Goodreads and/or Bookbub. It only takes a couple of sentences to say what you liked about the book.

Positive reviews are the lifeblood of an indie author, so please help us out! Thank you.

Also By CHUCK BUDA

Son of Earp Series

Curse of the Ancients

Haunted Gunslinger

Summoner of Souls

Desert Fangs

Corral of Blood

Redwoods Rampage

Stand Alone

In The Marrow

Sentinel Series

Sleeping Dogs Lie

Hangman's Noose

Gold Bug

Visit my website to find all these books, and more! www.authorchuckbuda.com

ABOUT THE AUTHOR

Chuck Buda writes across multiple genres including westerns, horror, and crime thrillers. He loves to eat pizza, drink whiskey and craft beers, listen to Norwegian Black Metal and search for answers about Bigfoot and UFOs. Plus, he works very hard to fit quotes from Seinfeld or Big Bang Theory into every conversation. That's a ton of fun in one man.

Chuck Buda and Armand Rosamilia co-host The Mando Method Podcast on Project Entertainment Network where they talk about all aspects of writing.

CPSIA information can be obtained
at www.ICGtesting.com
Printed in the USA
BVHW051135281122
652924BV00009B/176

9 781088 075265